The Real Blockwives Of Atlanta 2

A HUSTLER'S NIGHTMARE

SEVYN MCCRAY

Copyright

Playlist

Please enjoy the Real Block Wives of Atlanta Playlist on Apple Music. Featuring music created or featuring Atlanta Artists. https://music.apple.com/us/playlist/blockwives-ish/pl.u-06ox7rzsJjZZ7D

Dear Reader:

If you haven't been told that you are appreciated and cared about today, let me be the first to tell you. I'm beyond thankful to you for reading my work, whether this is your first or seventh novel by Sevyn McCray.
I sincerely appreciate you allowing me to take you on a journey away from your reality for a while.
I have been writing since I was in primary school. I wanted to transport a person to another place and time like I am when I put a book in my hand.
Writing about Atlanta is second nature because there is no place like home. I hope you have grown to love the characters I created. They are close to my heart and as real as it gets. Thank you and welcome to the Real Atlanta.
Peace, Love, and Blessings
Sevyn McCray

Acknowledgments

This is going to be short but sweet. Thank you so much for giving me a break, to my children, and to all of my readers... I love each and every one of you. Thank you for buying my books, reading my books, and telling others about my books.

As always... I dedicate this book to my brothers.... My lucky 7's. You are with me always, Dino (Big Puncho) and Randy (R.J.), and the man who made me his Capt. James E. McCray, Sr.

Prologue

"Jordyn, Jordyn, Wake up!" Chink shook Jordyn lightly to arouse her from the bad dream. She had already been tossing and turning all night, but when she started to cry in her sleep, he knew he had to wake her up.

She rolled over quickly and said, "Baby, I had the craziest dream." She then noticed that it wasn't Goldie sitting on the edge of the bed. Jordyn realized then that it wasn't a dream at all, and he was indeed missing.

Chink had not left Jordyn's side since she called him two weeks ago and informed him that Goldie was missing. He was scared, too. Jordyn had always been a ticking time bomb. His goal was to keep her from detonating. Her children had calmed her down over the years, but he knew who she was and what she was capable of. He had been around her practically all her life. That was why he didn't want to leave her, because there was no telling what she would do.

They were driving back to the club when they drove up on Goldie's truck on Peachtree Street, surrounded by police cars and a tow truck. He looked over at her, and he saw the tears in her eyes. She focused her eyes straight ahead as she pulled over and parked on the side of the street. Silence filled the car; neither said a word as they got out. When he squinted his already small eyes up to get a clear view, he saw what probably had made her start to tear up. The truck was riddled with bullet holes, and glass was everywhere. Chink shook his head and bit his bottom lip as they got closer. This did not look good because EMS wasn't in sight.

Jordyn cleared her throat as they got closer to the truck. A young man in a police uniform stopped them. He looked to be no more than twenty-one years old. He raised his arm to keep them from getting too close to the vehicle. She took a deep breath because, as usual, her first instinct was to pop off.

"Excuse me, sir, but that is my boyfriend's truck. He didn't come home, and I was on my way to the last place I saw him."

"I'm sorry, but I can't let you come any closer. This is a crime scene investigation. I will send an officer over to get your statement. You can sit back in your vehicle if needed, but don't leave the scene." He turned and headed to where the other officers gathered around the truck.

Chink looked at Jordyn as she looked at him. He wondered if the ambulance had already left the scene. He wanted to get closer so he could figure it out himself.

"But where is Goldie?" Jordyn asked as she turned around and headed back to the car. Even though she was fully covered, she felt a chill going down her spine. Something didn't feel right.

Chink opened Jordyn's door for her and headed around to the passenger's side. He didn't get back inside the car; instead, he looked over where the crime scene investigator's van had pulled up next to the truck. Two people jumped out and immediately began working on Goldie's vehicle. One was taking pictures, and the other was dusting for fingerprints. Chink twiddled his thumbs as he took in everything. His eyes slowly started scanning what was before him. He saw the shell casings, the blood, the tire marks, and the shattered glass. It appeared that Goldie might have been at the traffic light, and somebody pulled up beside him.

"Man, I need a blunt! What is taking them so long to come over here? They need to hurry up. I need to know what hospital they took Goldie to because it is obvious that he was shot. He is probably wondering where the hell I'm at," Jordyn said right before she put her hand up to her mouth to start biting her fingernails.

At least she was not in denial about something indeed taking place. They were raised under the code, 'Hope for the best, but prepare for the worst.' The same police officer from earlier was headed their way, accompanied by a female officer. Chink hated the police, so he got in the car. He would let Jordyn handle this. He was just here for moral support.

Jordyn looked over at Chink before she got out of the car to talk to the police. She hoped to draw strength from him but saw the uncertainty in his eyes. The look in his eyes mirrored precisely what she was feeling on the inside. The hairs on the back of her neck and the chill bumps under her sweater told her something wasn't right before the police even confirmed it.

"I want to apologize for my rudeness. I'm Officer Cato, and this is Officer O'Neal. She will be taking your statement. We are trying to set up a timeline of the events here."

Trying to remain as calm as possible, she took a deep breath before speaking. "Timeline of what events? What happened, and where is my boyfriend?"

"Ma'am, we are unsure. We were called to the scene after a report of shots fired and a vehicle accident. We arrived here and found the vehicle had crashed into the light pole, but no one was inside. We have found tire tracks that suggest it could have been a carjacking gone wrong. But we need to find the victim because he lost a lot of blood," the policeman spoke as if he thought that whoever was driving was still alive. The female officer had her notepad in hand, and she was taking notes.

"Find the victim; what do you mean by find the victim?" Mercedes shouted to the officers tearfully.

CHAPTER 1
Unexpected Expectations

Chrissy sat on the barstool, sipping from the small, blue bottle of wine as she watched Pretty prancing around the kitchen in the neon pink apron that said "Tongue Kiss the Chef." It was a beautiful Sunday evening, and her best friend came over to cook dinner and spend some quality time together outside of work.

"I hate to see women drink out of the bottle. Please pour that shit in a glass. That is unladylike," Pretty said as he cut up vegetables on the board.

"Bitch, I am in the privacy of my own home. I can lap this shit up out of a dog bowl if I want to. I should be able to let it all hang out as soon as I cross this threshold."

"Whatever, chile, practice makes perfect." He put the chopped vegetables in a sauté pan on the cooktop and turned it on before turning around and looking at his best friend with his hand on his hip.

"That is the difference between you and me, I don't have to practice being something I was born to be. Now, hurry up and finish cooking them damn shrimp and grits. I have been craving them all week," Chrissy said between giggles.

"Speaking of craving, you shouldn't even be drinking alcohol. You are expecting. Put that shit down before I be the one to tell your husband what is really going on." Pretty was excited, and he wanted Chrissy to have the baby. He felt that the baby would help keep Whyte from sticking his dick in these messy bitches that constantly played on Chrissy's phone.

"I'm just sipping. That won't hurt anything. The baby is only the size of a lima bean right now, anyway. I have only missed two periods. Chile, you act like I'm around here bussing out of my clothes. You'd better keep quiet anyway. Your loyalty lies with me. I wish you would tell Whyte anything. I would chop your damn head off." Chrissy laughed and put the bottle down for good. She didn't forget that she was pregnant. That was really all that she had been thinking about since she finally took the pregnancy test after vomiting every morning for two weeks straight.

"Girl, I'm going to be feeding that baby so much that it is going to come out looking just like me, then I'm gonna spoil her to death. See, I'm doing it already!" Pretty reached into one of the bags on the counter and pulled out three Maine Lobsters.

"You will become a full-time resident if you start cooking like this. Whyte and I are not going to let you go anywhere."

Chrissy didn't mind Pretty being over at all. She actually needed the company. Chrissy only saw her husband when he crept into bed in the middle of the night or first thing in the morning before leaving. She overheard him saying something about his incoming shipments, which had recently quadrupled in volume. She also knew that Goldie was still missing, so she didn't expect him to be home as much as he usually was. The stress was apparent because it seemed like he had lost weight in the weeks since Goldie's disappearance. Chrissy knew her husband was extremely fond of him. He was like the son that he never had.

"Will Whyte be joining us tonight? How is he holding up since Goldie has been missing?" Pretty asked, as he put the lobster in a pot of pre-seasoned boiling water.

"I was just sitting here thinking about him. I will call him and let him know you're here, cooking one of your gourmet meals. He needs to take a break from the streets and come home to a home-cooked meal, whether I'm the one who cooked it or not. He has been out there running himself ragged, and it is starting to show. It's Sunday anyway; this is supposed to be family day!" Chrissy reached into her purse, pulled out her cell phone, and called her husband. It went straight to voicemail. She left a message and then started texting him as well.

Pretty raised one eyebrow and directed his attention to the meal he was preparing. All he wanted was for his best friend to be happy. He knew all Chrissy ever wanted was a good home life and a successful business. She was among the sweetest and most generous people in the world, so he felt like she deserved it. He didn't want to overstep his boundaries and talk to Whyte, but he suddenly felt like something in the milk wasn't clean.

Chrissy's best friend was the only one that she had informed about her pregnancy. She didn't want children at the moment. She was focusing on her multiple businesses and her husband. But she knew that he wanted children. One of Chrissy's greatest fears was that she would turn out to be a fucked-up mother like her own. That was why she wanted to plan her pregnancy for the perfect time in her life. She didn't want to feel like she had missed out on anything and ended up taking it out on the child. That was one of her mother's main issues because she got pregnant with Chrissy during her last year in high school, so she never got a chance to do anything else with her life.

Whenever Whyte mentioned children, Chrissy would mention him hustling. His other businesses were successful, but there was something about the daily hustle that couldn't be duplicated behind a desk. The last thing she wanted to worry about was being a single mother. She didn't sign up for it. Suppose she was indeed going to have this baby. In that case, she would have to convince her husband that he could make his money grow legally and that it was indeed time to retire and hang up his jersey. She couldn't see that being done with one of his top earners and most loyal soldiers missing. Chrissy exhaled loudly as she thought about her life.

Pretty turned around from stirring at the stove. "Bitch, what is wrong now?"

"Do the other wives experience this problem as well? I know who I need to talk to... Mercedes! She has a daughter, and her husband is retired from the game. Maybe she could give me some insight 'cause I swear, I'm bout to pull my hair out."

"That's my bitch! I can call her right now. I think you two will get along well. She is so damn cool. If I gotta be bothered with two fishes, y'all are definitely the two I would like to be bothered with. Hell, do you mind her coming over this evening? Cause I know I can make that happen," Pretty said excitedly.

CHAPTER 2
Nothing Was The Same

"I swear I had almost a head full of hair last week. What the hell happened?" Mercedes said to herself, looking at her thinning hair in the bathroom mirror. Thank God for wigs. If she had strength after Chemotherapy, she could have bought herself a nice wig. She couldn't meet with clients and take care of business looking a mess. She had vowed to herself that she had cancer, but cancer didn't have her. Business was still business, and the show must go on.

Money walked into the bathroom behind her and kissed her on her neck. "What time do we have to be there, baby? I'm hungry as hell."

"Baby, you do not have to go to all of my appointments with me. I'm good. Don't you have some club business to take care of or something?" Mercedes appreciated that her husband was willing to do everything with her. She didn't want him to feel as if he had to put his business on hold to take care of her when she still had the strength to take care of herself.

"It's early. I have some deliveries this evening, but I can be elsewhere. I have employees, which is good, so I can be here for you. Baby, I told you we are in this together, so don't be trying to kick me to the curb."

"Okay, I just don't want you putting your business on the back burner. We started with a bang and are on top, and that is where we will stay." Mercedes turned around and kissed her husband on the cheek before leaving him alone in the bathroom. She knew he was going through a lot right now, even though he wasn't discussing it.

She had heard the bits and pieces of the conversations between him and Whyte. She felt him tossing and turning every night. Nothing had been the same since they left the club that night.

Money put his head down when Mercedes walked out of the room. He ran his hand over his bald head and shook it in disbelief. How could things be going so right and so wrong simultaneously? The club has been filled to capacity every night since the grand opening. Some of the most famous hip-hop and R&B artists have filled the schedule for the rest of the year. Luxurious was on the tips of tongues and ringing major bells nationwide. But then his wife was suffering from breast cancer, and someone whom he looked at as a brother was missing.

He felt helpless. This was the first time in his life that all the money in the world didn't mean a damn thing. Right now, being wealthy can't cure Mercedes' cancer or bring Goldie home. This realization hit him, and he pounded the marble bathroom counter so hard with his fist that pain shot up his arm. "Dammit," Money said out loud in frustration.

His phone rang, and the same unfamiliar number popped up. He pressed the Decline button. He didn't have time to entertain anything extra. Since he'd been interviewed in the Atlanta Journal-Constitution entertainment section, people had come out of the woodwork. His business cards listed his office phone number. If it were business, his assistant would handle it. His first priority was his wife and daughter. Money's phone rang again, and this time, it was Jordyn.

She sniffled loudly, "Bro, what's up? What you got going on today?"

"Shit, bout to head out to a doctor's appointment with Mercedes," Money said to Jordyn. He knew that she was going through it. He didn't know what to do besides what he was already doing, which was having niggas in the street trying to find out any information on Goldie or Dent.

"Wifey must be pregnant. You were heading to a doctor's appointment the last time I talked to you. Nobody goes to the doctor more than a pregnant woman." Jordyn tried to laugh at her joke, but it was caught in her throat when she heard Money's reply.

"Except a woman with cancer," Money said in a low monotone.

"Nooooooooo, please don't tell me that, Bro. I'm so sorry to hear that. I hope they caught it in time. And I thought that you had been moping around here because of Goldie. You are fighting your own battle. Man, I swear if it ain't one thing, it's another. If there's anything you need me to do, please let me know. I'm here for you all. I've been sending her a lot of business cause so many people asked about Goldie's outfit at the grand opening. I told them that she styled him."

"I appreciate that, sis. She needs to work; I think that is what's holding her together. Hell, Mercedes is taking it better than I am. She is receiving aggressive treatment. She had already started Chemotherapy when she told me that she had breast cancer. I want her to be as comfortable and happy as possible while she goes through this. She is a soldier. She is going to win this war. I feel it in my heart. We are going to kick cancer's ass."

"That's right! We just gotta stay prayed up and continue to think optimistically. I know my nigga is going to walk through that door. That is why I'm not planning any funerals or memorials. His punk ass momma popped up like a jack in the box. Talking about, we need to plan a memorial service for him."

"His momma? I didn't even know Shorty had any living parents. I never heard him talk about them. When he started hanging around Whyte, he told us he had been living on the street and spending nights at some of his homeboys' houses here and there," Money said, surprised.

"I know. I guarantee this bitch got an insurance policy on him. That is why she is trying to get him declared dead. Plus, she wants to get her hands on his belongings. I will sell that shit and put it in a trust for his children. His momma or his bitch ass baby momma ain't touching shit, and that is for sure," Jordyn snarled as she thought about the entire situation. These folks had just written Goldie off.

"Are you sure that it is Goldie's momma? These folks are so shiesty these days. She could be an impostor. It's not like we got somebody to tell us differently." Money had learned to be suspicious of people. Trust will get you killed.

"Unfortunately, it is. I don't know how his mama found out where I trapped, but I knew who she was as soon as I opened the door and saw her face. Goldie is the spitting image of her. I'm talking about twins, for sure. She had to have him when she was young. She looks like she is in her thirties."

"You know how the Westside is; she is probably in her thirties. She just jumped off the porch early. Hell, didn't we all? If she is that young, I guarantee you I know her. Didn't Goldie say he grew up in Flipper Temple and Hollywood Court?" Money said as he raked his brain, trying to imagine somebody who looked like Goldie from his past.

"Ain't no telling. I'm not going to hold you up. Tell sis I'm praying for her. Y'all hold your heads up and do some research on alternative medicine. Don't put everything in the doctor's hands," Jordyn said, ending the conversation.

"'Preciate it, Sis. We are praying for you and Lil bruh, too. I'll holla at you later, and if you hear anything, you know I'm a call away." When Money put the cell phone in his pocket and returned to the primary bedroom, the phone rang again with the same unfamiliar number. He took a deep breath and finally answered it.

"Yeah...Who dis?" Money answered the call, his voice full of exasperation.

"Nigga, it took you long enough to answer the call," his childhood best friend Biggs said from the other line.

CHAPTER 3
Something Gotta Give

Puncho rolled over, looked at his sleeping wife, and jumped out of bed. He grabbed his personal cell phone from the nightstand and entered the bathroom. It had been vibrating nonstop, and despite his efforts to ignore it, he couldn't. It stopped vibrating as soon as he closed the door, so he set it on the counter, plopped down on the toilet, and put his head in his hands.

Puncho couldn't deny that he was exhausted. In addition to his regular duties, he decided to help with the case concerning Goldie's disappearance. He wanted to be either on hand or a call away when any information was found so that he could handle it accordingly. He had to ensure that nothing found could implicate the organization.

The actual police investigation yielded no results. It was like Goldie had disappeared into thin air. But Puncho had his hunches. He couldn't shake the feeling that had been with him since hearing about Goldie's disappearance. His intuition told him that Dent had something to do with it, and he could not locate him either. The phone started to ring again.

"Yo, bro, sorry to wake you up. Julio just hit me up. The estimated delivery time is four hours away. I need you on hand to make sure that everything goes as planned. This is our biggest shipment from the West Coast so far. I need this to go super smooth because I know Ponchees is watching our every move. Can you handle that?" Whyte asked him.

"Yup, I got it. Is everybody else in place?" Puncho asked Whyte as he listened to see if he had heard his wife moving around yet. Since the grand opening, Tameka had been like his shadow for some odd reason. Perhaps she knew that he was aware of her relationship with the judge. Or it could be that she saw him in a different light now, having witnessed how he interacted with his friends. He shook it off as being just paranoid. She could only be under him and monitor his every move because she was no longer involved with the judge.

"One more thing, do you have anybody you can get to tail Head around? I thought about what you said the other night. I felt that he would lead us to Dent, and Dent would lead us to Goldie. I don't care what anybody says; I don't believe lil' bruh is dead."

"We just gotta stay optimistic. Something is bound to turn up, or something will come out. Niggas and bitches talk and trust and believe me when I say that I got my ears to the street," Puncho said to Whyte. Goldie was a good kid. He paid homage to his hood, cared for his kids, was loyal to his team, and was humble. Something definitely was going to turn up.

"Something gotta give because that damn Jordyn is talking crazy. Last night, she called me and said something about putting a price on the head of that whole set of Bloods. I talked her down, but I don't know how long it will last. Lil' sis is a beast, and she is in love with that young nigga. He got the right one riding for him, that's for damn sure. Alright, then, I'll text you about forty-five minutes before the time. I will see you later." Whyte ended the call.

Puncho washed his face, brushed his teeth, and opened the door slowly in an attempt to creep back into bed. When he opened the door, he saw his wife sitting in bed, waiting for him to come out. He wanted to close the door again when he saw the look on her face. He smiled, walked out the door, and returned to the bed under the covers with her.

"Don't come get in bed with that fake ass smile on your face, Jonathan. Who was that on your phone? Who in the hell is calling you this early in the morning?" Tameka folded her arms across her chest and huffed at her husband.

"Baby, calm down. That was only Whyte," Puncho answered honestly. He tried to keep it as honest as possible because he knew for a fact that lies always came back to bite you in your ass.

She smacked her lips loudly. "If that was Whyte, why did you have to get out of bed with me and go to the bathroom to talk to him?"

"'Cause the sun ain't even up yet, and I didn't want to wake you up," Puncho said, leaning over and kissing his wife passionately to shut her up.

Tameka broke the kiss. "Let me find out, Jonathan. Don't make me do something to you. I'm telling you it's going to take more than the Atlanta Police Department to keep me off of your ass."

"You don't have to worry about me cheating on you. What you don't give me, I take!" He pulled her back to him, aggressively kissed and nibbled on her neck, and worked his way down to her breast. He slipped the black teddy off her shoulders, which fell around her waist. He alternated from breast to breast. He was slowly sucking, nibbling, and licking her perfect breast as she started to moan softly.

Tameka grabbed her husband's head gently and cradled it as he sucked on her breast. She opened her legs a little under the cover as she felt her juices start to flow. Puncho knew how she loved to get her titties sucked. He knew that she was putty in his hands once he did that. She squirmed as he threw back the covers on them. When she looked down, she saw that his penis was on hard and pressing against his boxer briefs.

Puncho put his hands between her legs, and as usual, she didn't have any underwear on. He found her magic button with no problem, and he massaged it in a circle as he continued to suck and lick on her breasts. His wife moaned as her breathing quickened. She had already drenched his hand with her juices. He opened her legs wider and replaced his hand with his tongue.

Tameka cried out aloud. Louder than she wanted to, she hoped their son didn't hear them. She bit down on her bottom lip and hissed as he slipped a finger inside of her. When her husband started to suck on her clitoris and pump his finger in and out of her, the first orgasm hit her hard. She rolled her hips in a circular motion as he sucked and licked on her clitoris like it was a lollipop. Then, another one hit her harder than the first.

She tried to grab his head and bring it up, but he wouldn't let her. Puncho wrapped his arms tightly around both of her legs and locked down on her so she couldn't move. He flicked his tongue over her clitoris, soft and fast like an artist using a paintbrush. She hollered out his name loudly in ecstasy.

He jumped up before her orgasm subsided and entered her swiftly. Her tight fit always took him by surprise. Puncho bit down on his bottom lip and tried his best to get his mind off the tight, wet warmth surrounding his member. He knew he would explode fast if he thought about how good it was. He pumped in and out of his wife as he thought about who in the department he could bring into the fold. Then, all of a sudden, it got even tighter as her muscles clamped around him like a vise grip, and she started to rise from the bed, matching him stroke for stroke. When he looked down at her, the top half of her body was still lying flat, but she was moving the bottom half of her body in a way that suddenly had him in a trance.

Tameka moved like a belly dancer. Her eyes were low but focused on her husband's face. She watched as he bit down on his bottom lip and tried to concentrate on not bussing one in her.

"Come for me, baby. You can let go. Give it to me." She bucked on him even harder.

Puncho shook his head no as he closed his eyes as she did her mating dance on him. Suddenly, she stopped, and he opened his eyes to see that she had changed positions, and she was now taking his penis into her mouth.

"Fuckkkkkkkkkkkkkkkkkk," he hollered out as soon as she started to work her magic. He felt all the pent-up frustration starting to simmer to the top. When she took his entire length into her mouth, he felt her tonsils on his head, and that always drove him crazy. He could no longer hold it in. He exploded in her mouth, and usually, she would pull it out of her mouth and let it skeet on her breast, or she would take it in and spit it back out. This time, she swallowed every bit without taking her eyes off of him.

CHAPTER 4
Getting Out Alive

Chaney sat up slowly as the pain ripped through her body as well as her face. She didn't know how long she had been unconscious. The last thing she remembered was hitting Dude after he had sucker punched her in her face. She knew she probably shouldn't have started raining punches on him as he drove down the highway, but he had just verbally assaulted her and knocked one of her front teeth out of her mouth.

She panicked when she realized the car was on its side and all the airbags had deployed. After pushing the airbag away from her face, she looked to the driver's side and noticed that Dude was not in the driver's seat. Fear replaced the panic as she tried to unfasten the seatbelt; she had to find her husband.

So many thoughts filled her head as she unbuckled herself. Chaney had to get them some help. She fished around for her clutch to get her cell phone. It had slid in between the seats. She got it out and called 911.

"City of Atlanta 911, what is your emergency?" the female operator said.

"Yes, my husband and I were driving down the highway, and he lost control of the car, so we left the road. I just regained consciousness, but

I don't know how long I was out. The car is on its side against a tree. I had my seat belt on, but he didn't. He is no longer in the car. I think he was ejected through the windshield. Please send some help immediately. I'm scared to move because I don't want to make the car move, and I'm scared to stay in it because I don't want it to blow up. Please, please help us."

The operator could hear the panic in her voice as she pleaded for help. "Ma'am, do you have any idea where you guys are? Do you smell any gas or hear anything leaking?"

"I don't smell any gas or hear anything leaking. I'm not sure where we are. We got on the highway at Spring Street going south, and I think we were on the highway for about ten minutes before the accident. Would it help if I told you that the headlights are still on and that a large metal pole is in front of the car? I think that it is a billboard." The evil thoughts that she was thinking about her husband had disappeared and were replaced with prayers as she hoped that her husband was okay.

"Yes, ma'am, that helps a lot. I'm dispatching police officers in that direction. Please stay on the line with me and remain still. They will have their sirens on, so please let me know if you hear them. I can let them know that they are in the correct area," the operator told Chaney before she started firing off rapid instructions over a police radio.

Her heart was beating wildly in her chest, and it seemed that every breath that she took filled her with pain from her face down. She was straining to keep her eyes open; Chaney wanted to close her eyes so badly. If only she had just waited until they got home before she started in on him. There she was again, doing what she always did, taking the blame for something she didn't create.

Dude started the argument, he hit her first, and this was his fault. She kept telling herself that quietly as she waited patiently for the police to rescue her. Her husband had manipulated her already insecure being and had preprogrammed her to accept responsibility for everything that went wrong.

She remembered how he blamed her for the reason he was cheating. It was then that he made her stop talking to all of her old friends. He knew that they were her eyes and ears in the street. He was the one cheating, but he didn't want to let her out of his sight.

Chaney knew she wouldn't be in this predicament if her friends and family were still around. Her mother never liked Dude, no matter how well he took care of her. The first time she met him, she said he had an evil spirit and was hiding something.

She would go home to see her family if she made it out of this situation alive. They only knew she was still alive because she sent money home. She needed her momma to hug and tell her everything would be okay. Her eyes drifted closed, and the phone slipped from her hand.

* * *

She pulled up, and the valet parked at the Mandarin Hotel; she had planned a girls' day for her friends at the spa inside the hotel. She was excited to be out from under her husband. She had been missing her girls. Ever since he made her quit the club, he acted like she couldn't even go in there unless she was with him.

He didn't understand her when she told him these girls were more than her coworkers; they were like her sisters, and she missed them. Chaney didn't know what getting married would be like, but she sure didn't imagine it would be like this. She had just found out that she was pregnant. That was all that her husband talked about, his first born son. Dude just knew that she was carrying a boy.

Ever since she told him that she was pregnant, he had not touched her sexually. She was frustrated; she wanted to ask her girls if it was normal. Hell, in her mind, nothing Dude did was normal. She woke up this morning and wanted to call her mom to share her good news, but she didn't, because she knew that backlash would come from it. So, she decided to spend time with her friends instead. She knew they could make her feel better. Chaney could imagine their faces when they got the group text she sent out as soon as her feet hit the floor this morning.

"Meet me at the Mandarin at noon for a spa day. Love y'all bitches, miss you more. I will see you later."

What she thought would be a bonding session between her and her closest friends turned out to be just the opposite. They told her everything they had been hearing about her husband. Of course, Chaney told them they were mistaken when they said to her that her husband had been going to Onyx and Magic City for years, trying to get the baddest chick to fall for him.

"Girl, I have been dancing since I came to Atlanta five years ago and started at Magic. I remember when Dude first exited prison; he always came in with his boys, Whyte and Money. He never used to get any dances; he just sat there looking out of place while they got dances. He didn't even have dreads, he had a baby fro, his teeth were fucked up, and he had bad acne and everything. I have no reason to lie to you. I love you, girl. I tried to warn you when you started messing with him, but you wouldn't listen. Back then, it was just rumors, but some of this shit I have seen with my own eyes, and I've heard it from the horse's mouth. That nigga is gay. You are just a Beard. That nigga don't want no pussy no more than I want some pussy, and you know for a fact that I don't mess with women at all."

Chaney sat frozen in place in the sauna. If someone touched her, she would turn into a pile of ash. She wanted to cry, scream, and take off running, but instead, she lashed out at her long-time friend, Debbie Cakes.

"You're just mad because you're thirty-seven years old, and you are a grandma and still stripping. You mad cause ain't nobody rescued your ass yet. You don't have to badmouth my husband because you obviously can't get one. My nigga might be many things, but he ain't gay!"

"Y'all calm down, don't start to attack one another. We've been down for too long for some bullshit to come between us. Now Sweetie Pie, you know Deb wouldn't come to you with no bullshit. I've been hearing shit, too. You've got to open your eyes, girl. This is Atlanta. It is bitches around here that look better than us, finer than us, and everything, but they got dicks. They ain't playing fair in this city. Take heed before you learn about this shit the hard way. We love you, and the reason why we haven't come to you yet is that we didn't want to be coming to you on no, he says, she says shit. I know for a fact that what she is saying is true. I've seen Dude with a tranny before, and like I just said, I've heard a lot worse. Don't let the dollar signs blind you. Just be careful. These folks ain't playing fair, and I don't want you to be a casualty of his madness."

She stood up and looked at her two friends; her insides, including her heart, felt like they were melting. All she wanted to do today was spend

*quality time with them, have girl talk, and tell them about her baby. But
that wasn't the case. Chaney was hurt, and instead of letting her friends
be there for her, she let her hurt get the best of her, and she exploded.*

*"Don't know, Sweetie Pie, me bitch to soften the blow. You sound like
you are jealous, too. For all I know, one of you bitches could be fucking my
husband on the low and throwing this other shit in the game to keep the
heat off of you. I don't have time for this shit. All of you bitches stay here
and enjoy yourselves on my husband. Good riddance!*

*"I'm going to let you have that cause you mad, but trust and believe
you will need me before I need you. I'm many things, but one thing I'm
not is a hater. Just tell ya, ol' man, to strap up when he is fucking you, and
put some extra condoms in his wallets, so his boyfriends can strap up when
they fucking him," Debbie-Cakes said to her Chaney"s back as she walked
out of the sauna.*

*Chaney cried all the way home; this was the last time she saw her
friends. She didn't even tell Dude what they were saying about him. In her
mind, she believed what they were saying was true. Their sex life was
unlike anything that she had ever experienced.*

*She went along with it to please her husband. But with the accusations
and the fact that he hadn't touched her since she found out she was pregnant, she didn't know what to believe. She prayed that it was all in her
head and that there wasn't any truth.*

*This was why he didn't want her to be around her old friends; he kept
her close to him or alone, so she couldn't make any new ones.*

"Ma'am, Ma'am, can you hear me?" A police officer had exited his
car, walked down the embankment, and shone his flashlight inside the
vehicle. He only saw one person in the passenger's seat. She appeared to
be unconscious. He got on his radio and told the operator that the
victim was unconscious, and he was told to stand by because more help
was on the way.

The helicopter circled the scene, illuminating the woods with its
bright lights. The car was severely damaged. He hoped that this young
lady would survive. Her chest rose and fell, so she was still alive; he
didn't know for how long. He returned to his radio and informed the
operator that the car was severely damaged and needed help immediately. He fought the urge to try to take her out of the car by himself.

CHAPTER 5
Biggs Back

Money, Biggs, and Peppermint sat in the car outside of Major's spot. Money had watched him like a hawk for the last two weeks. His friends were always down for any money move, so he knew they would come along for this. He wasn't a taker, but they were.

Money felt bad because he made this seem like just a random lick. But deep down, he hated this nigga to his core. Major was the biological father of his girlfriend Mercedes' baby. His old ass had taken advantage of her and threw her away like she was a piece of trash.

"I'm surprised he doesn't have none of his bodyguards with him. You know he never goes anywhere by himself," Peppermint said from the back-seat as he popped another soft peppermint into his mouth.

"He is never in the public by himself. But he comes home by himself every night. This is where all the money is. This will be a piece of cake," Money said to his homeboys.

"I thought you said this is where he kept the dope and the money. I only came to get the work," Biggs said from the passenger's seat. He had just gotten out of Fulton County Jail and needed to get back on his feet. He'd been gone for three months, and it took all the money he had put up to pay *for a lawyer and his bond. Rubbing his hands together, he thought of how he could get the nigga to give up where the work was.*

"You a fool, you get the money, you don't need the dope. Major is supplying everybody with all the work right now, so trust me, you will be set for a minute. You already know that he is sitting on a big sack." Peppermint said, smacking on the candy.

"I know he is; he walks in the house every night with a full backpack on his shoulder. I've been watching this nigga. Nobody ever comes to visit; he has no burglar bars or anything. There is nothing but old people who live on this street, which is a dead end. This time of night, it's abandoned; you won't even catch a car coming or going down the street. I'm telling you this is going to be easy as pie. When he turns off the television, that is when he is going to bed," Money informed them.

"He turns off the television, goes to sleep, then what? This nigga ain't about to just let us in if we go knocking on the door. You've been doing your homework on the nigga, so you have come up with an idea on how to get in. I'm not used to going inside a house when the people are still there. I don't do home invasions; I do burglaries," Biggs said as he pulled a pack of Newport 100s out of his jacket pocket.

"Don't smoke that in here; I got asthma," Peppermint said, handing him candy.

"That is what Peppermint is here for; you know, if he can't do anything else, he can pick a lock and a pocket. Trust me, I have thought of everything, we straight." Money sat back in the seat and waited for the television to finally go off so they could go off in Biggs' crib.

* * *

2 HOURS LATER

Peppermint put his lock-picking kit back into his army-fatigued jacket pocket, turned around, and signaled for Money and Biggs to join him. They quickly came up on the porch with ski masks pulled down over their faces. As soon as they got inside the ranch-style house, they looked around, and it was nicely decorated.

It looked more like a family home than a single man's home. They tip-

toed lightly on the shiny hardwood floors so as not to make a sound. Money spoke of the backpack, which was still on the leather sectional sofa. Peppermint looked at it and then at Money, who signaled that he should go ahead and pick it up.

He opened it up, and his eyes got big when he saw all the bankrolls of cash rubber banded in what he presumed were bundles of a thousand. He gave Money a thumbs-up sign, closed it, and threw it over his shoulder.

Money tiptoed to the bedroom, where he believed that Major slept. When he opened the door, it was a child's room. In the middle of the full-size bed was a little boy sleeping. He closed the door slowly and cursed himself silently. He wondered how he had missed this significant detail.

He had never seen Major with any children, nor did he see any going or coming in the last few weeks that he had been watching the house. Biggs came up behind him, and he whispered to him.

"Man, it's a little boy in there sleeping. I've never seen this nigga with no children. We need to dip."

"No, we don't nigga! You said he was asleep. We are about to go in here, wake this man up, and make him go in his safe. Then we will leave." Biggs walked around Money toward the next bedroom with his Glock 40 in his hand.

Money exhaled deeply as an unsettling feeling came over him.

For some odd reason, it suddenly went from feeling like nothing could go wrong to the uncertainty that everything could go wrong in the blink of an eye. He looked back toward the child's closed bedroom door before he followed behind his friend.

Biggs opened the door slowly, hoping the old plywood door wouldn't make a sound to wake the sleeping man. He crept across the floor slowly to the king-sized black lacquered bed where Major lay sleeping on his stomach. Loud snoring filled the room. He looked up, and Money was on the other side of the bed with his pistol at his side. Despite the ski mask on his face, Biggs could see the fear in his eyes.

Money's hands sweated, and his heart was pounding in his chest. He took a deep breath one last time, trying to shake the feeling of doom that had overtaken him. Right now, it wasn't even about the money that he was going to walk away with; it was about doing something to this nigga whom he despised.

Major had taken something from Mercedes that she would never get back, so his taking this money was only retribution for the unjust act. He deserved to take some loss. Money raised his pistol, leaned over, and put it up to Major's face.

"Wake up sleeping beauty. We need your help." He shook him awake with his other hand.

Major moaned loudly and opened his eyes. When he saw the assailant standing at his bedside with the pistol pointed in his face, he started to roll over quickly. That was when he heard the cocking of another gun.

"Be easy my nigga, we don't want any problems. We just came for the cash, and nobody will get hurt," Biggs said from the other side of the bed when he saw Major making an abrupt movement.

"Y'all dumb ass niggas passed by the cash on the way back here. It's in the front room on the sofa in the book bag. Get that shit and leave up out my muthafucking house," Major said, with dried-up saliva around his mouth and crust in his eyes.

"Oh, we got that already. We need that cash out of the safe. Now, get up slowly. If I catch you flinching, I'm gonna blow your brains out your head." Biggs looked over at Money as he stood as still as a statue. This was his lick, but now he was acting like he was scared.

"Ain't no safe in here. Who in the hell y'all think I am? Scarface or something. I ain't nobody. Y'all made a mistake. I'm just a single father, trying to stay out of the way and make enough change to take care of my momma and my son. Take the book bag and leave; it's about nine or ten thousand in there.

"We know who you are. We did our homework. Now, I'm gonna tell you one more time, get up slowly, so we can open the safe," Money said as he gritted his teeth. He was perspiring under the ski mask, but it wasn't because he was hot. His gut never misled him, and he felt like everything was wrong.

The hair stood on his neck as his eyes darted around the moonlit bedroom. He was on edge because he felt something was about to pop off for a reason he could not explain.

Slowly, Major rolled over on his back, rose from the bed, and swung his legs over the side. He was quietly trying to plot out his next move. He wondered to himself how many others were in his house. He prayed that his son stayed asleep.

He had been in the game since he was twelve and had never been robbed. That was something he prided himself on. He was going to have to take off these niggas heads because he knew that he wouldn't be able to live that down. If they got away with robbing him, then it would officially be open season on him and he wasn't about to let that happen.

"Get the fuck up! The quicker you open the safe, the faster we can be out of your hair. This is not all you got, so go ahead and come wit it. You probably have accounts overseas. We are not hurting you by taking a little bit of your re-up money," Biggs said as he raised his pistol higher and came around to the side of the bed where Major was currently standing. He cocked it loudly in his ear to let him know that he was not playing with him.

"Since y'all niggas think that you have done your homework, then you know that you are not going to get away with this. My young niggas will kill you just for sport. If you do this, you are putting a target on yourselves and everybody you associate with. I see you taking your grandma to church; she is a target. I see you talking to a girl at McDonald's drive-thru; she is a target. I see you with your children; they are targets. I'm Major, and I do not take losses. Take your girlfriends to the movies, them bitches targets, too. You take from me, I'm going to get it back tenfold, and I'm going to get it in blood."

He just wanted this shit to be over, so he pushed him in the back of the head. "Man, shut the fuck up and open the goddamn safe. We didn't come here for all the threats," Money said as he started to walk toward the bedroom door.

"No threats, straight promises my nigga. Trust me and I put this on everything that I love. I don't fuck with nobody, but when I fuck with a muthafucka, I fuck them to death or at least till they can't take no more of my fucking with." Major headed down the hall to the living room, where he had the safe. Wishing like hell with every step that he took that he had put his pistol under his pillow. It was just his luck; he had left it in his car because he knew he had his AR-15 under his bed. He didn't think somebody might get to him before he could reach under the bed. What he had

in the safe was not just a little re-up money. He had over two hundred thousand in it. He only emptied it once a week.

Money looked around, but he didn't see Peppermint in sight. He was probably in the child's room making sure that he didn't wake up and come out and see his father being robbed. He locked eyes with Biggs and watched as he mouthed, "Where is Peppermint?" He hunched his shoulders.

They went into the living room, and Major walked toward a large canvas on his wall, which was of the pyramids of Egypt. He lifted the picture off the wall and took a deep breath as he put it on the floor. His heart was pounding in his chest; he was hoping that this would not be a night when his son woke from his sleep and came to get in the bed with him or that his mother would come downstairs from her tiny apartment that he had built upstairs in his attic to check on his son or clean up like she often did when she couldn't sleep.

Major focused on opening the safe so he could get them niggas out of his house. He would have to pain them in the streets. He straightened his back and knew that right now, it wasn't about the money but about making sure nothing happened to his son or mother.

Biggs watched him slowly put the combination in the safe. He was paying attention to Major's every move. He never really heard anything about him in the streets other than he was getting money; he heard of no beef or anything. There was something about his eyes that didn't look right. He was gritting his teeth and his temple was jumping; he was boiling over on the inside. There was a clicking sound and then a pop and the safe came open slowly.

He eased up so close to him that he was sure Major felt his breath on his neck. He cocked his pistol and put it deep in his side. Money didn't want any false moves; his nerves were on edge, especially since he didn't see Peppermint. A door creaked slowly down the hall, and he switched his attention toward it, and everything changed in the blink of an eye.

He snapped out of his reverie when he realized Biggs had repeatedly called his name. Money looked up and saw his wife puking into the container. "Nigga, I thought you said that you couldn't get no cell-phones in there anymore. You must have started banging fucking with another correctional officer?"

"Nawl, nigga, I'm at my sister's house. I'm home. Come holla at me," Biggs replied.

CHAPTER 6
Second Guessing

G oldie woke up groggy. He tried to open his eyes, but he couldn't. They were swollen shut. The very act of trying to open his eyes made his entire face hurt. His shoulder no longer ached; it felt numb from the right side of his neck to his fingertips. The last thing he remembered was getting hit on the back of the head when he got smart with one of the niggas as he was being stuffed into the truck. From the way that his face felt, he was sure that he had been beaten.

With his hands tied behind his back and his feet tied together, he tried to get as comfortable as possible on the bed. At least he wasn't on the hard floor; he wondered where they had taken him. His stomach growled loudly. He was already a little nigga; he didn't need to miss any meals.

Goldie was mad because he couldn't open his eyes to tell if it was night or day. He had no idea how long he had been unconscious. What a way to end what he thought was the best night of his life. He had planned on proposing to Jordyn when he got home to add the icing to the cake, and now this shit. He cleared his throat; it was so dry. He needed something to drink, too.

The sound of a door opening slowly interrupted the silence. He heard footsteps and then what he presumed was a chair sliding across the wooden floor. Then he heard breathing and smelled Kush and cologne; it dawned on him that they had not blindfolded him. That meant that they didn't care if he saw them because they wouldn't let him make it out of there alive.

"So, you thought I was just going to let you get away with taking my family and friends away from me that easy? Nawl, you ain't no dumb nigga so you couldn't have thought that," Dent said as he looked at Goldie tied up on the bed. The blood from the gunshot wound had soaked through his shirt and jacket and had pooled around him. He had lost quite a lot of blood; he was praying that he didn't wake up. The blood had dried, and you could smell it faintly in the room.

Goldie had thought that the assailants were someone Dude had hired to come for him. He had been on pins and needles since he walked in on him and the punk. He knew that Dude played dirty and wouldn't want that information to get out and tarnish his reputation.

Never in a million years did Goldie think that Dent even had it in him to pull off something like this. He really didn't have the guts. He wouldn't have done this without this crew of new niggas that he was hanging with.

He opened his mouth to respond to Dent, noticed how dry his mouth was, and cleared his throat. "Aye, can you untie me, so I can at least go and use the restroom and get some water?"

"No, I'm gonna let you lie right there and rot." Dent slid the chair back, got up, and walked out the door, slamming it.

* * *

Head saw Dent walking up the hall with his head down as if deep in thought. "Everything good Blood? You decided how you wanna end this? I don't see why y'all didn't just end it right then. Now you gotta worry about his people searching for him. I don't care what you do as long as it doesn't bring problems to my front door or my operation."

"I want the nigga to suffer, and I want the bitch to suffer wondering is he alive or not. You don't have to worry about it. I got it, Big homie,"

Dent said to Head as he wondered how he was going to end Goldie's life. He had never killed anyone before and he figured if he had to murder someone to get in good with Head that it might as well be the nigga that he hated the most.

"You gonna have to do more than shoot a nigga in the shoulder and let him starve to death to get in good with me. I need to know that you got heart," Head said as he popped the cork on the black bottle of champagne.

"I'm the one who shot the man in the shoulder. Dis nigga never even took his gun off safety," One of Head's foot soldiers named Turtle said as he came into the living room of the house that he ran.

Dent bit down on his bottom lip and looked out the corner of his eye toward Turtle. He watched him as he sat on the edge of the sofa and started to roll a blunt. Head must have forgotten all the information he had been giving him daily on Whyte and his organization. He began to say something, but he didn't. He would just bid his time; he knew it was coming. His primary focus was to take Goldie out. He wasn't worried about Whyte and the rest of them. That was Head who had the beef with them.

Head burst into laughter. "You're gonna need somebody to hold your hand through each step, I see? Ummmmm, this might be why you never worked your way up the totem pole when you were on the other side. Don't make me second-guess my choice to bring you on."

There was a knock at the door, and he answered it to divert Head's attention from him. It was Raquel; she was there to see Turtle. Dent's eyes got big when he saw her through the peephole. He knew that they were kicking it, but he figured that he would've chosen to meet up with her somewhere else since they were now holding her baby daddy captive in this house. He turned around and said, "Aye, blood, the girl Rock at the door for you. You want me to tell her that you ain't here, right?"

"Nawl let da bitch in; she knows I'm here. I was texting her and told her to pull up." Turtle lit the blunt and hit it. Then he stared at it as the smoke invaded his lungs. He started coughing loudly because he had been holding it in too hard. His eyes watered, and tears rolled down his face as he tried to control the coughing from the potent weed.

"Dats that pack right there, ain't it?" Head questioned his homie. He had just gotten a new batch of weed in. He didn't smoke himself, so he always looked to Turtle to try the weed first because he was a weed connoisseur.

"I hadn't gotten a chance to open that up yet. I got this from some nigga name Chink from the Westside. I've been hearing a lot of people talking about it. Calling this shit "Rapper Weed".

Hearing Chink's name made Dent's ears shoot up like a dog.

"Chink? Dat big pussy ass nigga. I can't stand him. Bae, don't buy shit else from his punk ass. He is always cheerleading for dat bitch Jordyn," Raquel said as she walked in the door past Dent. She tooted her nose up at him and looked him up and down.

"Aye, watch your mouth, lil' mama. Ain't no use of making no enemies where it ain't needed," Dent said as he poked his chest out proudly. He could talk about Jordyn all day long. Still, he refused to let anybody else speak negatively about the mother of his kids. Because regardless of what they were currently going through, she still had been there for a nigga.

"Damnit, man! I mean what da fuck? Dis bitch must got some good ass pussy cause it seems like every nigga in Atlanta want to save this ho'. Are you still under her spell? It might have worn off since she left you high and dry for my baby daddy. You should hate her more than me. I mean, shit that was your friend. Y'all in the same clique of niggas. I know you feel salty about that. That's probably why you over here with my new nigga. Your old crew didn't have any more respect for you after you let a nigga ten years younger than you scoop your bitch right from under your nose." Raquel reached over and got the blunt from Turtle before sitting on his lap.

Head watched the exchange in silence. He saw Dent opening and closing his hand as his temple jumped. His eyes had narrowed as he tried to control his anger. Ol' girl was getting out of pocket. He hoped that Turtle wasn't trying to wife this lil' young ho because she didn't know how to act accordingly. Now was the time she was supposed to be seen and not heard.

He exhaled loudly, "Yeah, every real nigga wants a prize, a trophy, something that he can be proud of. Oh, you wouldn't know anything about that. You never have and never will fit into that category." Dent twisted all the locks on the door and went outside to get a breath of fresh air.

"What da hell was that all about?" Turtle asked as he got the blunt back from Raquel and patted her on her back as she choked off the 'Rapper Weed.'

"Looks like you need to do some homework, lil' bro. I'm bout to head out and go and get B.G. from majorette practice. Her nanny had some personal business to tend to. I will take her out to eat and to the mall. I will hit you niggas up later. Hit my line if anything comes up. Oh yeah, I hope you got your antennas up cause it some shit going on and we need to be ahead of the game like always.

CHAPTER 7
Money Talks

He sipped on his cranberry juice and lit the blunt as he twirled around in the executive chair behind his desk. It was something about being in his office that always calmed him. It could be because it showed him how far he had come or because he was away from everything that was going on. Money was worn out mentally. His wife's illness weighed heavily on him, and now Biggs had gotten out and worried him. Not to mention, he was concerned about everything surrounding Goldie's disappearance.

He had not gotten a good night's sleep in God knows when. The first night that Biggs got out, he went to his sister's house, sat for a while, and gave him five stacks to shop for a new wardrobe. But then the following day, he called him so that he could take him to the mall.

Money didn't have time to babysit his friend. He was too busy focusing on his business and his wife's health. He was happy that his long-time friend was finally home, but there was something in his gut telling him that this was going to be more than he had bargained for. He had yet to tell Mercedes that Biggs was home.

Money had long ago stopped talking about Biggs when Mercedes found out that Biggs was locked up for the home invasion that resulted in Major's paralysis and his mother's murder. He didn't want her to ever find out that it was he who set the lick up. He made it seem like he didn't know what Biggs was really locked up for. When his wife found out how much he was doing for Biggs, she said, "I wish I had a friend like you. But she thought he only did it for birthdays and Christmas. She didn't know that he was sending that amount of money to him every month.

Money felt that was the least that he could do. Biggs let him get away with murder. Thinking about it always took him to the darkest place. He didn't want anybody to die, not even Major. He just wanted him to suffer. It wasn't a day that went by that he didn't think about his friend Peppermint. Then the fact that Major's mother died during the whole melee was something that never left his heart. That was one of the reasons he tried to put out all the good that he could because he had sown so many bad seeds in such a short time.

He looked up when Whyte walked into the office. He stepped lightly, but Money felt someone approaching. They had that kind of connection. "I was trying to hide for a minute."

Whyte burst out laughing loudly as he took a seat in the chair in front of Money's desk. He had his own office in the club, but hardly ever went to it. He always just made himself at home in Money's office. Money was the brains behind the club. He loved everything about the nightlife.

"Well, you shouldn't have come to work. Everybody knows where to find you, my boy."

"I'mma be honest, I think it is just something about the condo. It seemed so big, but now with Mercedes being sick, it seems small. I think it is time we looked into getting a house on some land. The condo in the sky seems to be suffocating me. It's like trapped air up there or something. I smell the sickness as soon as I walk in the door. The smell would be contained if we were in an actual house." Money's face was screwed up as he could still smell the scent that he was trying to get away from.

Speaking of sick wives. One of the chicks that I fuck around with is a nurse at Grady. She said that Dude's wife is in critical condition. She was in a car accident. I had been so caught up in my own shit that I hadn't even realized that I hadn't talked to him. Have you heard from him lately?" Whyte said as he got a bottle of water from the mini-fridge.

"I thought he was out of town doing something with the music. I'm used to him disappearing. However, I know that you speak with him regularly, whether he is in town or out. I haven't heard from him or seen him since the night the club opened. Well did you ask ol' girl if he was in the hospital too? When did this happen? Why hasn't he gotten in contact with us?"

"She said that she heard through the grapevine that she was found in a car on the side of the road. She had been there for some days," Whyte said.

Money pulled out his phone and started calling Dude. Even though he already had a lot going on in his life, he tried his best to be his brother's keeper.

"Ain't no use in trying. I have been blowing up Dude's phone since I found out. It's going straight to voicemail," Whyte said; he was filled with worry, too. He had told her to find out as much info as she could on Chaney's condition and to see what she heard about Dude.

"Well, it's ringing now; I wouldn't be surprised if he is out of town working and doesn't know what is going on," Money said, hoping for the best. The last thing they needed was another person from the organization missing.

Whyte took the fact that Dude's phone was ringing as a good sign. He had planned to visit Chaney after checking in with Money. He knew his friend had a lot going on with the new business and his wife's recent diagnosis. He missed Money having his hand in the game because he helped ensure everything ran smoothly. He promised himself he wouldn't say anything about the illegal business. Whyte planned on trying his damnedest to keep Money an honest man.

"How is Julio liking the West Coast? I haven't been able to talk to him much since he moved to Cali. We both are so busy, and the time difference doesn't help. Lord knows I miss my boy being right here with me. It feels funny. You know we are damn near attached at the hip."

"He is doing well. I'm happy he was willing to go out there, especially since he suddenly fell in love with your wife's best friend. She made the move easier because she willingly travels to see him every weekend. So, he is doing the long-distance relationship thing." Grateful to have solid people on his team, Whyte expanded nationwide with no problem.

"Yeah, Dejah seems to be head over heels already. I don't know what happened that night in Luxurious, but I can tell you everything changed for everybody. She is a good girl; she definitely has her head on straight. She is a beautiful doctor with no kids, and she is from the trenches. Hell, it's like he designed her himself." Money loved Dejah like a sister and wanted her to be happy. It helped that she connected with one of his friends, who he knew was the perfect match for her.

"Those were his words exactly," Whyte said, laughing, getting up from his seat.

"You know you have your own office across the hall, right?" Money asked sarcastically.

"I got an office at the studio, too, but I don't go in it either. The streets are my office," Whyte said as he exited.

CHAPTER 8
That Dude

D ude didn't know who to call first when he activated the new phone. He had been watching the news since he checked into the W hotel. So many things were going through his mind. He had not seen a story about Chaney's accident on the news yet. Maybe something was shown when he dozed off. The Percocet, Xanax and syrup mixture had him leaning badly. He could hardly keep his eyes open. He hoped she was dead, and then all he had to worry about was what he was going to do to Goldie. He had to shut him up before he started to talk.

The pain he was feeling in the beginning had started to ease. He couldn't imagine how he even climbed out of the car. Dude knew that he was moving strictly off adrenaline. He was in so much pain the first night after the accident. But the bruising and swelling in his midsection seemed to be getting worse. Maybe all the meds he was on were masking the pain. Dude knew he needed to put something on his stomach before he ended up overdosing.

Chelsea walked into the room with two plastic bags loaded with food. She put the food on the table, walked over to the bed, kissed Dude on the cheek, and ran her hand over Dude's locks.

"Are you feeling better, baby?"

He looked over at her and admired her beauty. It wasn't even ten o'clock, and she looked like she had just stepped off the runway. Everything was flawless, not a hair out of place. Her designer clothing fit all her curves as if they were made for her, and her face looked like an artist had sculpted it. You would never know that Chelsea was born a man. Dude didn't have a problem with Chelsea being born a male; in fact, he liked it better that way. He was living the best of both worlds.

Now that Chaney was no longer in the picture, Chelsea was happy. She had stopped blackmailing Dude. He didn't know that she didn't plan on outing him because she had a lot to lose as well. The people in Atlanta didn't think she was born male.

She was designing clothes and was about to open her first brick-and-mortar store, despite having achieved great success online for years. She was moving in the circles that she wanted to move in, living the life as a woman, and she had finally gotten a man who loved her and wasn't trying to use her or expose her for being born as a male. Moving to Atlanta was the best thing she could have done.

"I was just thinking that I needed to put something on my stomach before I take anything else for the pain," Dude said, his voice slurring.

"Great minds think alike. I got all your favorites." Chelsea got a plate off the table and piled it with fruit, cheese, eggs, French toast, chicken sausage, red potatoes, and onions. She sat beside Dude on the bed and fed it to him slowly. She had vowed that when she picked him up on the side of the road in the middle of the night weeks ago that she was going to use this time to nurse him back to health, get to know the real him outside of clubs, the trips, the sneaking, the freaking.

He finished eating, and they lay in bed in silence. The silence was getting to him; his mind started to wander. Dude wondered why no one had found Chaney in the ravine yet. He knew the area was wooded, but he thought one of the helicopters flying over might have spotted it by happenstance.

Whether she was dead or alive, it would have made the news. A missing person's alert would have been put out for him if Chaney were alive. Something told him he needed to check in with one of his partners. He would learn everything he needed to know just by how the conversation went. Dude looked at the new phone on the nightstand. He had activated it, but then he turned the power back off. He wasn't ready yet.

Chelsea wanted Dude to come home with her. She recently purchased a new construction home six months ago and had yet to bring a man home with her. After this time together, she knew that this was the man she wanted to be the first to sleep in her bed with her. She leaned over and untied the drawstring on the Diesel pants she had just bought him. She pulled them down and lowered her head and freed his limp penis from his boxers. He was still sore, but that didn't stop her from doing what she knew she did best.

Dude inhaled and felt a sharp pain, but the pain became dull as he concentrated on the warm wet mouth that was wrapped around his dick tightly. He bit down on his bottom lip and hissed loudly as he looked down and saw Chelsea's blond head going up and down slowly on his member. But what drove him wild was when she started to slurp, moan, and deep-throat his dick.

His toes curled in his socks. Everything he was thinking about at first emptied from his mind as he placed one hand on Chelsea's head and the other behind his head. Dude was now totally relaxed. He glanced out at the beautiful view of the Atlanta skyline. There wasn't another place that he would rather be.

She did not care if she had to suck his dick for hours on end; she was going to make him fall in love with her. He said he forgave her for black-mailing him, but she had to make sure. Chelsea made it her business to be on her best behavior; she had not asked him for a dime since he called her to pick him up. The accident was a blessing in disguise; it was just what she needed to get close to him as she had wanted to. She was paying for the hotel, she went shopping for him, she was waiting on him hand and foot and giving him bomb ass head, day in and day out. He would be putty in her hands when it was over.

Chelsea looked up and saw that his eyes were closed tight. She slobbered all over his dick and started to jack it off. She put his balls in her mouth and alternated between sucking them. Dude opened his legs wider as he moaned like a bitch getting her pussy ate. Chelsea stuck two fingers in his asshole quickly, and he grunted and moaned. She knew that he would much rather this be her dick, but he was still too banged up for her to be having sex with him like that. This would have to do. Her main priority was to keep him satisfied sexually, and she knew she was doing the job when he started moaning louder.

"Damn baby, this shit feels good. You make a nigga feel like he's on top of the world." He felt like he was about to bust. He started humping her face, and she shoved her fingers in and out of his ass. He let out a loud growl as he came. Chelsea swallowed every drop of cum, got up, smoothed the invisible wrinkles out of her jumpsuit, and headed to the bathroom.

She looked at herself in the mirror and smiled. She had come a long way in a short period. Everything was falling into place. She had a consultation with a doctor about having the last procedure that would make her a full-blown woman. She was excited and didn't tell Dude. Chelsea brushed her teeth, freshened up her makeup, and left the bathroom.

"Baby, you think that your people can get you some more pain pills. I think I'm ready to travel. You figured out where you wanted to go yet?" Dude winced in pain as he tried to straighten himself in the bed.

"Yeah, I can bring you something back. I haven't really thought about where I want to go. How about we go to my house? It's almost seven thousand square feet, full of new furniture, and empty. You can't stay cooped up and hiding," Chelsea said as she picked up her purse and headed toward the door.

"I was just thinking that, as well. I'm gonna call my partners and business associates to make sure everything is good and we can go to an island for a week, and when we get back, I will come home with you." Dude yelled out in pain as he tried to reach for his cellphone. He got it and started to power it up. A coughing fit overtook him. Chelsea brought him a bottle of water from the mini fridge and headed to his side. Blood was on his hand when he reached for the bottle of water.

"Oh, my God! Baby! Your mouth is bleeding!" Chelsea shouted in panic.

"No, it's coming out of my mouth. I'm bleeding internally. Call 911," Dude said before he passed out.

CHAPTER 9
Left For Dead

She opened her eyes slowly, and when she did, her mother stood at her bedside. A smile slowly spread across her face. Chaney hated admitting that she hadn't seen her mother in forever.

Tears sprang from her mother's eyes as she grabbed her hand and dropped to her knees slowly. "Thank you, Jesus. Thank you, heavenly Father," she shouted loud enough for the nurse walking down the hall to hear and peek in.

"Amen!" she said as she walked into the room and witnessed the mother getting up slowly. She was smiling, but her face was streaked with tears. The nurse got her stethoscope and listened to the young lady's heartbeat. She then checked her monitors. Chaney's vitals had doubled since her mother had been at her bedside. The nurse shook her head and thought about the power of the praying mother before reaching for her phone to call the doctor and let him know that his patient was awake.

Chaney reached up slowly and removed the oxygen mask from her face. "Where is Dude? Is he here also?" She had on a neck brace, and she couldn't look around the hospital room. She wondered how long she had been unconscious. The last thing Chaney remembered was being in the car, turned upside down on an embankment.

"Nawl, dat nigga ain't here. There is no telling where he is. I hope his dirty ass somewhere in dem woods dead," her mother said, her voice dripping with venom.

"Don't say that, mother. He is still my husband. I can't help if you don't like him," Chaney whispered.

"I have very valid reasons. I've told you from the beginning that Dude wasn't right. I bet you my last five dollars that he had something to do with the reason why you are lying here in this hospital bed. I told you the first day that you bought him to Augusta that nothing good would ever come from him. I hope this is the sign that you need. You could have died, Chile, and then I would've been locked up for murder. Cause I will kill that nigga about mine."

"Mother, calm down before you get your blood pressure up. The last thing that I need is for you to be stroking out. If I'm laid up, who will take care of you? I need to talk to the authorities to find out what they are doing about finding my husband."

"You don't have to call them. They are bound to turn up. They have been coming down here twice a day since you were admitted, according to the nurse's report. They think that you have some crucial information. Now, do you want to tell your momma what happened that night when you were driving home?"

"Can I at least have some water first?"

She poured a small cup of water for her daughter, got a bendable straw, and put the straw between her lips.

The liquid in her mouth felt so good. Chaney swished it around first before swallowing it. She finished the small cup in three sips and took a deep breath before talking.

"We went to this big party, and we were on the way home and got into an argument. I said something that set him off, and he struck me. My tooth fell out my mouth, and then I went crazy on him and started beating his ass. The next thing I knew, we were leaving the road. I woke up a little while later, and the car was on its side, and Dude was gone, and so was the windshield."

"A little later? No, try three days later. You were in that embankment, trapped in that car for three damn days!" Chaney's mom sat down in the chair beside the hospital bed.

"No way, I was only in the car for a few hours. It was dark when the accident happened, and it was dark when I woke up."

"Yes, it was dark, but it was days later. God was with you down in that ditch. Just think, you woke up long enough to call the police, and then you fell unconscious again. That was nothing but God. You are the first thing I pray for when my eyes open in the morning and the last thing I pray for before my eyes close at night. Keep my child safe, dear Lord. Keep your arms of protection wrapped around her tightly." She reached up, grabbed her daughter's hand, which was hanging off the side of the bed, and rubbed it soothingly.

Tears ran down Chaney's face as she thought about how she was in the car all that time and how anything could have happened to her. "What have they said about Dude? He was probably still out there deep in the woods, hurt. He went out the windshield. This is Georgia; we've got coyotes, wolves, bears, and all kinds of stuff out there. Something could have eaten him up."

"Quiet as it is kept, your husband is a vulture. Vultures don't eat other Vultures. Something in my heart tells me your husband isn't in the woods."

Chaney shifted in the bed slightly and took a deep breath. She wished she could turn herself over to look out the window. She wanted to look anywhere but the ceiling as the tears fell from her eyes slowly. Despite what she said, she didn't feel that her husband was in any danger in her heart either. She had a flashback.

"Bitch, I should leave you. You are nothing but dead weight anyway. I'm a millionaire. I can make a life anywhere with anyone. Who wants you? You are a washed-up, uneducated stripper. I'm the only person who wants you."

"He left me, Momma; he left me for dead," Chaney said in a voice so small that you had to strain to hear it.

43

CHAPTER 10
Help Needed

"**M**y nigga, what is going on? I've been calling you like crazy, and you haven't answered. Did they tell you that I came to your club last night? I was in that bitch turned up with some niggas that I met when I was locked up in Macon State Prison. They are from Summer Hill. I'm proud of you, my nigga. It was packed from wall to wall. That joint is niiiiiiiiice. You are doing big things," Biggs said into the phone as he side-eyed Dee.

"I'm happy that you enjoyed yourself. I'm going to throw you a little something to welcome you home. I just am so busy, man." Money was lying on his chaise lounge in his living room, watching television with his daughter. He really didn't feel like talking to Biggs. He was trying his best to hide his irritation.

"I know you say you're not fucking round no more. But I was hoping you could do me one solid, and I promise I won't ask you for anything else. I need the plug. I got my own money. I saved one of them country niggas lives, and he just gave me enough to get me at least two bricks. Put me on, bro." Biggs was lying through his teeth, but he knew that he could come up majorly with the connect and the money that Dee promised him.

"I told you I don't mess around, period. The club is the only thing that is making me money. I'm on the straight and narrow. But if I hear of anything, I will let you know. I still keep my ear to the streets. You be safe out here, bro. Shit ain't the same no more." Money looked up and smiled as Mercedes came out of the kitchen carrying his plate of food. Today was a good day for her. She was full of energy and had a smile on her face.

"Damn, bro, you ain't kicking it with me no more? You won't give me the plug. Don't fall off that high horse. Remember, I was the one who helped you get up there," Biggs said, feeling some way because it seemed like his old friend wasn't messing with him anymore.

"Nigga, you free. If you need cash, I can help you. If you need a job, I can help you. But two things I'm not about to do is kiss your ass or babysit you. My wife got breast cancer, and I just opened a new business. I don't got time for shit else, but what the fuck I be doing. You understand me."

Biggs gritted his teeth. He held back what he really wanted to say as so much of his past flashed before his eyes in less than sixty seconds. He lived in his nephew's old room at his sister's house. He didn't have a wife, and he didn't have any kids. His mother died while he was in prison, serving a sentence for a murder he didn't commit, and this nigga had the nerve to try to chump him off. Now, he didn't feel bad about what he was about to do. Hell, Money didn't feel bad about him rotting his entire adult life away in a prison cell.

"Yeah, I understand you loud and clear, bro. I'm praying for your wife."

Mercedes wanted to ask her husband who was on the phone, but she could tell that the call put him in a bad mood. She got up, fixed him a double shot of Hennessy, placed it on the end table, and sat silently across from him in front of the television.

The doorbell rang loudly, startling Money out of his reverie. Heavyn got up from her beanbag and headed to the door.

"What in the hell is up with the concierge? They do not call anymore," Money said irritably.

"Baby, calm down. Whoever it is has to be family if they let them right up." Mercedes joined Heavyn at the door before she opened it.

Money picked up the glass and downed the shot in one big gulp. Biggs had thrown him off. He was in here raising his voice at his wife and she damn sure didn't deserve it. He looked up, and Jordyn was standing there with tears streaming down her face. Right then, everything that he was going through seemed small, even the cancer. Money got up and wrapped his arms around her. She burst into tears.

Mercedes saw this and her eyes watered. Her husband had been telling her how hard Jordyn seemed to be taking Goldie's disappearance. She pulled her daughter closer to her, wrapping her arm around her waist. In situations like these, you had to pray for the best and prepare for the worst.

"Hey girl, I just cooked. Can I fix you a plate?"

"I haven't eaten in God knows when; I might need to try. Sorry for interrupting you like this. I can't sit around and twiddle my thumbs. We have all this money, and we can't find my man. The police don't seem to be doing anything, but we have one on our team. I need something. I haven't slept three hours straight in I don't know when. I need Goldie here with me. I need some answers. It's too many questions and no answers."

"What do you want us to do, lil sis? I will run with whatever suggestion you have. If you've got a plan that is well thought out, I'm game." Money hated seeing Jordyn like this. She was still hustling, so she needed her head all the way in the game.

"I was picking up my lil' sister from school yesterday, and a red G-wagon caught my eye. When I got close to it, I saw it was that nigga Head. His daughter goes to Southwest Christian Academy with Destiny. So today, I decided to follow him. I know where he lives; I know where his daughter goes to school," Jordyn said as Mercedes put a plate piled high with collard greens, macaroni and cheese, beef pot roast, cornbread, and squash on her lap on top of a silver serving tray. She looked down, and her mouth watered.

"Okay, so what are you going to do with that little bit of information? I know the wheels started turning in your head. We must think out our every move. We are trying to win the game."

"By any means necessary," Jordyn said as she started to stuff her mouth full of the delicious food Mercedes had cooked.

Money got up and went to the kitchen to reheat his food, as it had cooled since his wife had set it in front of him. He wasn't with the 'By any means necessary.' He wanted Goldie home safe, but he was still living with the consequences of shit he did years ago. He couldn't go down that road again. He bowed and said a silent prayer that Goldie was still alive. That was his greatest fear.

Jordyn ate the food as if it were going to be her last meal. She used the last bite of cornbread to get all the crumbs and juice left over. She popped it in her mouth and looked up shyly when she noticed Mercedes watching her.

"That was so good girl. I see why my brother married you. You cook like somebody's grandma." Jordyn could cook, but didn't think her food was this good.

"Yeah, I hit the lottery with her," Money said as he walked back into the living room and took a seat on his chaise. He watched as his wife took Jordyn's plate from her and left the room.

"I got a plan, bro. We can kidnap his daughter. We will give her back when he gives us Goldie," Jordyn said as soon as Mercedes was out of earshot.

Money leaned his head down in shame because he had a daughter. There was no way in the hell he was about to kidnap anyone's child. "Now, sis, I know you want Goldie back. Hell, I do, too, but we can't take somebody's child. What do we do with her if, God forbid, Goldie is dead? Kill her, too? I'm not fucking with nobody child!"

"But bro, he ain't dead. Don't you think if he were dead, I would feel it? I know he is alive! If you don't help me, somebody will. I came to you first because I knew you would be in my corner." Jordyn had yet to tell Chink about her plan. She knew he would help her; he had never said no before. She got up and looked at Money. She had more tears on her face than when she entered the door.

He didn't know what to say. Money watched her walk out the door in silence.

CHAPTER 11
New Connections

Chrissy moved around the shop in silence. Pretty could tell something was wrong, but he didn't say anything. He knew that when she was ready to talk, she would. That was one of the reasons why they got along so well; he picked up on all of her vibes.

She exhaled loudly as she plopped down in the chair beside his station. "I don't have any more clients. I'm going to go ahead and leave for the day. Call me when you are finished to discuss the pop-up shop booked for tomorrow night." Chrissy's frustration would not let her sit in the shop all day and watch Pretty work.

"Where are you going bitch? You bet not leave me here slaving on the farm picking cotton. I want to leave, too," Pretty said, pouting his big lips and batting his long lashes at Chrissy.

"If you don't be still. You got all those damn customers out there. That is what your greedy ass gets. You are the one who doesn't want to hire another stylist because you want all the money. Now you are stuck here. Just call me. I think I'm about to go shopping. That always helps me relieve some of my stress."

"You better not step in one damn store without me. Bitch, you are so damn petty. Why are you doing this to me? I've been shopping for you for ten years. You don't have one piece in your closet that I didn't pick out. You know you need me, chile." Pretty enjoyed dressing Chrissy, he was her unofficial stylist. She got to wear everything that he always wanted to wear, especially now that she had plastic surgery. Her size was perfect for her height.

"I got the perfect shopping companion, and she does it for a living. See you later, babes." Chrissy blew Pretty a kiss before leaving to pick up Mercedes.

"Oh no, you don't! You'd better tell Mercedes that I don't about you. She can't have my other half." Pretty got a good vibe from Mercedes, but he didn't want her to be bosom buddies with his best friend. Since they all had dinner together that night, Pretty saw they had formed a close bond.

Mercedes' energy levels were high today. She had just gotten off the phone with Dejah. She was sad because she no longer had any time for her. She was either working or jet-setting across the country to be with Julio. Mercedes never would have thought that all that playful flirting at the grand opening of Luxurious would have turned into a full-fledged bi-coastal relationship. This was the time that she needed her the most. Thank God for Chrissy. She had just fallen into her lap, and they hit it right off.

Mercedes walked out of her building and put on her sunglasses. She flipped her hair over her shoulders and strutted in her Chanel wedges. The custom wig from the Hairbortory in L.A. made her feel like herself. This burst of energy she had over the last few days, combined with the new hair on her head, made her feel cancer-free. She inhaled the fresh air, pulled her shades down on her nose, and looked around. She didn't see Chrissy's truck; in fact, she didn't see anyone, yet she felt like she was being watched.

She shrugged off the feeling when Chrissy pulled up to the curb in her husband's Range Rover. Mercedes hopped in, leaned over, and hugged Chrissy and kissed her on the cheek.

"Girl, I thank God for you rescuing me. I swear, some days I'm walking around the condo like a zombie. I started looking at furniture last night. I need a change or something. It seems like it is so small to me all of a sudden. We seem to be living on top of each other. I'm getting claustrophobic."

"Honey, that is all in your head. I remember seeing the condo when you first closed and was impressed with its size. Come on now, it's just the three of you there. You act like you have a house full of people. You might need to move the furniture around." Chrissy said as she headed toward the highway.

"Anyway, enough about me. What's on your mind? I could tell over the phone that you have something going on. Where is your truck?" Mercedes wondered aloud as she adjusted her seat, removed her shades, and put them in her purse.

"Damn! Am I that transparent? Pretty just asked me the same thing before I left the shop." Chrissy couldn't shake the uneasy feeling that she had been having. She still hadn't told her husband that she was pregnant. Whyte was in the streets so much that he probably didn't notice.

"I don't think that you are transparent; it's just that we have a connection. So tell me, what's wrong?"

"You and Money have been together all y'all life. Do you ever worry about him cheating on you? Like when he was still hustling in the streets, did you ever think he was out with women? Am I just being paranoid?" Chrissy asked just above a whisper. She was apprehensive about opening up to someone. Still, she knew that if anyone understood her plight, it would be Mercedes.

"I'm going to be honest if a nigga is going to cheat, he can be in the boardroom or the dope trap. It doesn't matter. When you are dealing with boss-type niggas, even if the nigga ain't a cheater, you got to worry because women throw pussy at them left and right. Then you know Money was in the clubs promoting way before he opened his own. I try my hardest not to even think about it because you can drive yourself crazy.

I love my husband and only have eyes for him, but I'm not delusional. I want him to respect our union and our family. If Money is cheating or has cheated, I don't know anything about it. Bitches have never approached me, and I have never heard anything." Mercedes was happy that she could say that with pride.

Chrissy knew Whyte loved her. He was the only man she had ever been with and wanted to be with. But with the streets come hoes, so she wanted her husband out of the streets. "I'm pregnant," Blurted Chrissy.

Mercedes's neck snapped so fast when she turned to look at Chrissy driving. She could tell by the way that she said it that she wasn't happy with her prognosis. She and her husband wanted a baby. Some folks have all the luck. "Well, at least it ain't cancer," Mercedes tried to laugh it off.

Chrissy immediately started to feel guilty. Tears began to fall from her eyes. "Here I am complaining when shit could be a hell of a lot worse. I'm sorry, girl. I'm so stupid. It's bitches that would kill to be me right now."

"You're right, but do you really think Whyte is cheating with someone? You know he is the head of the operation, and his workload has increased recently. Julio has moved to the West Coast to handle the new business, Money has retired, Dude seems to be all about the music, and Goldie is missing," Mercedes said solemnly.

Chrissy hadn't looked at it like that. What Mercedes had said was true; she knew her husband had a lot on him, but she was still suspicious. "We are about to see!"

CHAPTER 12
Self Check

Money didn't know what was wrong. Maybe he was missing the streets; it could be his wife's cancer or his homeboy missing. He couldn't put his finger on it. He had to check himself. He was snapping off on everybody. He had been feeling bad ever since he told Jordyn that he wouldn't help her kidnap the little girl. He had not even talked to her since then. He took his phone out of his pocket and dialed her number as he walked out on the balcony of the condo. Jordyn didn't answer. He left her a message telling her to call him as soon as she could.

Then he called Biggs; he hadn't talked to him since he blasted him. He didn't want to get wrapped up with Biggs again, but he did feel like he owed his old friend. Money wished that he had asked him for a lump sum of money, a car, or something tangible. Just like the night of the robbery, Biggs always wanted to touch the dope. It reminded him of Whyte; he always has to be hands-on and in the thick of the streets. It was the rush of adrenaline that came with hustling.

"Aye, Bro, what's happenin'?" Biggs said when he picked up. He was salty with Money, but he still needed him to set him up with some work, so he played it off.

"Shit, standing out on the balcony. Wish I was blowing one right now. A nigga don't have any weed at the house," Money said happy that Biggs sounded like everything was alright with them.

"You probably can't keep weed in the house with wifey having cancer. I heard it's good for them."

"Mercedes is a prude. I told her weed was good for her. She is not fucking with it, but she do everything else green. Drink green tea all day. She is even growing grass in the house that she drinks. She will not hit a blunt, though."

"You gotta look it up and show her. I saw a special on *Dateline* about how it helps with pain, appetite, sickness, and a whole lot of other things. Maybe she thinks you just bullshitting trying to get her high," Biggs laughed.

"I'mma do that because after chemo, she's gonna be messed up. I feel so bad for her. Where are you, bro? I'm getting ready to head to the club; come blow with me, and I'll get the chef to fix us something to eat. Today is the first day that we are doing the happy hour mixer for the singles."

"I'm with that, I might need to put on a shirt and tie, get me one of those corporate chicks from down there on Peachtree. I'm getting tired of these young hoes that keep throwing themselves at me, all they want is a nigga sack. I haven't even made it yet." Biggs was hoping to himself that he could talk Money into hooking him up with Whyte. Dee was getting on his nerves, threatening to lock him back up if he didn't make anything happen soon.

* * *

"I wish Peppermint were here with us. He would be proud of you, bro. You have come a long way from selling them break down dimes that you got from Bowen Homes. I see why you say you're here every time you turn around. I would be, too. Being here means seeing all of your dreams come true. If I were you, every time I walk in the door, I would be pinching myself. I wonder how we would've turned out if you never put us on that lick that night," Biggs said as he refilled his glass with the Dusse's cognac as they sat in the V.I.P. area of the club.

Just hearing Peppermint's name sent chills up Money's spine. It seemed like whenever he thought of him intentionally, he didn't think about the robbery or how he was killed. But when someone else brought it up, he always went back to that horrible night when everything had gone so wrong.

As soon as the safe popped open, Money's eyes lit up when he saw the stacks of bills piled neatly, along with two watches, a ring, and a large necklace. He didn't come for all that, but he decided they would take it anyway. He looked over his shoulder and instructed Biggs to grab the backpack and fill it up with the money from the safe.

"I don't have it. Peppermint picked it up before he went to the back of the house," Biggs said as he moved in closer to get a better look at the contents of the safe.

Major instantly thought about his mother and his son. He hoped whoever was in the house with them wouldn't harm them. "Your folks better not put one hand on my mother or my son. I swear to God."

Just as he said these words, Peppermint walked into the living room behind an older woman who was ambling slowly. Money's eyes bugged out of his head when he saw that Peppermint had a gun to her head. The lady was wearing a robe and had rollers in her hair; tears were running down her face as she sniffled loudly. He shook his head; how could he not know that this man's mother and son lived in the house with him? Shit was going all wrong.

"Momma, you all right? Where lil' man at?" Major called out as he faced toward the safe.

"Antonio, who are these men? What do they want? Whatever it is you have, give it to them, baby. God don't like ugly; he will punish them and return your blessings one hundredfold," the older lady said to her son, her voice shaking with fear.

"I'mma give it to them momma, but where Lil' Man at?" Major asked her again.

"I thought he was in your room with you," she answered.

As soon as she finished her sentence, there was a noise coming from the back of the house that startled them all. Money turned his head, taking his focus away from Major, who turned around and ran toward his bedroom. Biggs fired shots toward Major, hitting the floor and the wall as he scampered on the floor out of their view. His mother turned around and pulled a small .22 caliber pistol out of her robe's pocket, stuck it in Peppermint's chest, and pulled the trigger. He didn't see it coming because he was too busy looking at the little boy in the hallway. Money fired one shot at the old lady, and she fell to the floor. Peppermint was still standing, but his shirt was quickly filling with blood.

Money stood rooted to that one spot in shock. He couldn't believe he had shot someone and someone's mother at that.

"Hurry up, we've got to get the hell out of here," Biggs said to his two friends. He was wondering what type of nigga Major was; he ran and left his mother there to fend for herself.

Peppermint started gasping for breath, and he pointed to the little boy in his pajamas in the living room. He was coming toward where his grandmother lay on the floor in a heap with a pool of blood starting to form around her.

Hearing Peppermint breathing so loudly snapped him out of it as he rushed to his side just before he passed out. Money caught him and tried to shift him so that he could carry him. Biggs got the knapsack, emptied the safe into it, and kept peering toward the back with his pistol drawn.

"I'm stronger than you. Let's switch." Biggs threw Peppermint over his shoulder and gave Money the knapsack filled with cash and jewels. They headed toward the front door. Money looked back, and the little boy was sitting on the floor right next to his dead grandmother, watching their every move, but there was no sign of Major.

They made it to the car and placed Peppermint in the back seat. This time, Biggs got behind the wheel and Money sat on the passenger's side.

"We gotta hurry up and get him to Grady. We can pull up and leave him in the emergency room. I know he will keep quiet about what happened. We will come and see him tomorrow," Biggs said as he drove fast through the quiet neighborhood.

Money was turned around in his seat, looking at Peppermint, who seemed to be losing a lot of blood. "You gotta hurry, man, he's bleeding so much back there." He felt his friend's pulse, and it seemed to be weak

Biggs was worried about his friend and wasn't paying attention when he ran the stop sign. He was happy no cars were coming through the four-

way because that would have been an accident. He thought everything was okay until he heard the sirens and saw the flashing red and blue lights in the rearview mirror. "Oh shit!"

"You think that you can outrun them?" Money said nervously as he looked back and saw the police car pursuing them.

"I can lose them if I hit the back streets." Biggs knew all the backstreets like the back of his hand; it came in handy when he and Peppermint were out doing their thing.

"Okay, well, hit 'em then, bro. We gotta get our boy to the hospital, quick, fast, and in a hurry." Money wanted to crawl into the backseat with Peppermint to ensure he was okay. He felt so guilty. He was the one who got them into this in the first place.

He quickly turned off Collier Road and turned off the car's lights. He then made another turn onto a rocky road. Biggs was happy. He thought he had gotten away because he no longer saw the flashing lights. The flashing lights reappeared as he was about to come out at the end of the rocky road. The street ahead was blocked out with what looked like multiple cop cars.

Biggs threw the car into reverse, and as they approached the way they had come, he saw more flashing lights. He looked, and Money was looking at him, panicked.

"You just need to get out and run. This way, when they get me and see Peppermint in the backseat, I can say I was rushing him to the hospital. They will call an ambulance and get him immediate care, and if I get locked up, you just come bail me out in the morning. Okay? Do we have a deal?"

"You sure?" Money asked as he looked at Peppermint in the backseat. He had his hand on his chest, and his hand was covered in blood. His eyes were closed, but he could tell that he was still alive because he could hear him breathing and see his chest rising and falling with each breath.

"Yup, that way, we are clear about everything else that happened tonight. I got your back, bro. Always and forever," Biggs said as he slowed on the dark rocky road. He just hoped that Money would be able to find his way through all of the woods.

Snapping his fingers in Money's face. "Aye, bro, you see that one that just walked in? She is bad, and I mean that in a good way. I'm about to get the waitress to send her a drink over."

Money snapped out of his reverie. If it weren't for Biggs taking that case all those years ago and being responsible for Peppermint, he wouldn't be standing right now. If all he wanted was the plug, that was the least he could do. He would double whatever he was getting to give him a good start. "What were you saying, bro?"

"Man, you are still the same, always daydreaming. I was saying that I'm going to send the girl that just walked in a drink, and then I'm going to go and introduce myself," Biggs said as he adjusted the collar on his button-down.

"Sounds like a plan. But let me run something by you right quick. I have decided to assist you with the request you made last week. You still want to do it, don't you?" Money saw Biggs's eyes light up like a Christmas tree as he started cheesing showing damn near all of his teeth.

"Yup, I haven't spent a dime. I got enough to buy two bricks of Coke." Biggs said, wanting to jump out of his seat.

"I'mma do you one better to make it right. I will double whatever you get and introduce you to my folks so you can handle business with them from now on." Seeing the excitement on Biggs's face made him feel better.

"You will do that, bro? Aww, man, thank you. I have a question. Don't you miss it? The hustle? I mean, there is no way you are making the type of money in this club you were making in the dope game."

"I'm doing something that I always wanted to do. I was selling dope as a means to an end. I got enough money; it's about the satisfaction of doing something I always dreamed of. You are the one who used to burglarize houses so that you could buy dope to sell. You liked being the dope man for some reason ever since we were kids. You like the dope game, bro. I always wanted to be a businessman with a house full of kids and a fine-ass wife. But I'm still hustling, however. I'm just hustling these clubs. I think I'm about to open up another one soon in Miami. It won't be as large, but it will be on the main strip."

"I dig it, bro, and I appreciate everything," Biggs enthusiastically said as he rubbed his hands together. He hoped that the wire he wore picked up on everything being said.

"I got ya back always and forever. I am my brother's keeper," Money said as he put the Dusse in the glass before him and lifted his hand to summon the waitress.

CHAPTER 13
He is the reason

W hyte tapped on the partially open door lightly. He waited for a minute, and then, when he didn't get an answer, he walked inside quietly. The hospital room seemed colder than the rest of the hospital. It was filled with silence and despair. There wasn't a get-well card, a flower, a balloon, or any semblance of brightness that usually decorates the hospital rooms. Her head was bandaged up, and her back was turned to him. He watched as her body rose and fell with each breath she took. He turned around and walked out.

Walking toward the elevator, he thought about his wife, his backbone. Guilt filled him as he thought of how he had not spent time with her lately. The new workload and West Coast expansion had taken up much of his time. He was short of many hands that were usually there to help him, but Chrissy should be the last to suffer the consequences. Whyte's phone vibrated as he got on the elevator. It was the nurse whom he had recently met. He had told her he would call her when he got to the hospital. Whyte shook his head and exhaled loudly before entering the gift shop. He had to do better; women were his weakness.

Whyte knew he was fucking up. He had to find a way to make it right, because he knew his wife had to feel even worse if he felt this way.

"Can I get some assistance with the items I'm about to purchase? I need them delivered to room 483 on the fourth floor."

The teenage girl came from around the counter, and Whyte stopped and glanced at her for a minute. She reminded him so much of Chrissy when he first met her. His guilty conscience was whipping his ass. He busied himself by picking up greeting cards, candy, and flowers. He pointed to a giant teddy bear, and when he reached the register, he ordered ten helium-filled "get well soon" balloons. Whyte picked up two books as well and pulled out a bankroll.

"This will be all. How soon can you deliver these things to room 483?"

"Sir, I can bring them up as soon as my relief comes on duty." She took the money and counted it. It was too much. She handed him back six crispy twenty-dollar bills. He shook his head and smiled.

"No, that is for you," Whyte told the young lady who came from behind the cash register and hugged him.

"Thank you so much. I will get this upstairs as soon as possible. You have a blessed week, sir," she said joyfully.

Whyte got back upstairs in record time. He tapped on the door lightly, and just as he was about to open it, it opened for him. Chaney stood on the other side of the door, bent over slightly at the waist, holding the doorknob.

She looked at his face, and his eyes seemed to twinkle, but his expression stayed the same. Chaney sighed heavily, opened the door wider, and allowed him to enter. She was searching for a feeling or intuition to kick in and tell her why he was there. He was the only person who had come to see her beside her mother. She laughed at herself because she realized she didn't have anybody else. She had run everybody else off. If Whyte was here, where in the hell was her husband?

"Dude sent you?" Chaney asked as she limped slowly back to the hospital bed.

Whyte watched her silently as she shuffled along, not even picking her feet up. He didn't know what to say, so he answered her question.

"No, I don't think he knows you are here. What happened? How long have you been in here?"

She plopped down on the bed hard and shifted her weight before adjusting the bed so that she could sit up properly. Chaney was still in extreme pain. She didn't want to be doped up all the time. Out of all the people, it had to be Whyte who came to visit her. She watched as Whyte pulled up a chair close to her hospital bed. Her room suddenly felt different. She became self-conscious; her hand instinctively went to her head, as if to do something to her hair. She quickly forgot that her head was wrapped up like a mummy.

When Whyte said that Dude probably didn't know she was here, it was all she needed to hear. It was like the final nail going into the coffin. "He does know that I'm here. He is the reason that I'm here. He left me in that ravine to die. But it wasn't my time. God has something great planned for me. I was supposed to be dead; I was on the side of the road for three days. I might be walking slowly, but I will walk up out of here. Better than I was when I was with him. Everything happens for a reason, and I'm not even bitter."

"Wait a minute, wait a minute. I'm confused. What happened?" Whyte was trying to process what Chaney was saying, but none of it made sense to him.

"We argued on the way home from the grand opening. He hit me and knocked my tooth out. I started hitting him back. The car left the road. I woke up days later, still in the car. It was on its side in a ravine off the highway. Dude was nowhere to be found. The police searched the area and came up with nothing," Chaney said as she looked at Whyte for some reaction.

He was in absolute shock. He couldn't believe his homie was going out like this. If he didn't want to be with Chaney anymore, all he had to do was walk away. You don't try to kill a person. Dude always acted strange when it came to women anyway, but he thought that maybe he had changed with his wife because she was beautiful and intelligent and seemed to be down for him. This was the longest relationship that he ever had.

"On the side of the road? Where? Are you sure they searched well? If the car was on its side, he could have gotten ejected from it and been out there dead in the woods."

"That is what I thought. The police searched high and low. We went through it, but I didn't think Dude would throw me away like trash. My friends were right all those years ago. He has been using me all this time." Tears start to pour from her eyes as reality sets in.

Whyte felt so bad for her. He thought about how Dude was before he got with Chaney. Chaney definitely made Dude a better man. When he got with her, all those rumors that started to surface when he was released from prison stopped. Then he thought about what she had just said, when she accused him of using her. Whyte tried to push the thought from his head. There was a light tap on the door.

"Come in," Chaney said as her eyes lit up when she saw two people coming in the door pushing a cart loaded down with flowers and stuffed animals. It had at least a dozen balloons tied to it. Maybe Dude had realized what a mistake he had made. She looked at the door to see if someone else was coming in behind them.

"I appreciate that, Miss Lady. Here you go." Whyte handed the other person, along with the young lady who had helped him earlier, a twenty-dollar bill as a tip.

Chaney was happy and sad at the same time because, for a brief second, she thought her husband might still love her. "All this is for me? You shouldn't have."

"Yes, I did. I walked in here, and you were sleeping, and it felt like a hospital room," Whyte said as his phone started to vibrate. He looked down and saw that it was Money calling him.

"It is a hospital room, silly." Chaney laughed playfully for what seemed like forever. She couldn't remember the last time that she had laughed.

CHAPTER 14
Nobody Goes Harder than Me

ordyn paced back and forth with the blunt in her hands. The ashes were falling on the floor, but she didn't care. She had just gotten off the phone with Puncho, and he said the police didn't have anything new. She felt like they were half ass doing their job, and she didn't want to take her anger and frustration out on her friend, so she ended the phone call as fast as possible.

The tears started to fall from her eyes while she was on the phone with him. Lately, it seemed like she couldn't stop. She didn't understand how someone could just disappear into thin air. She was talking about Goldie, but she was also referring to Dent. No one had seen him either.

Chink walked into the living room with the duffle bag over his shoulder. He sat it down on the floor and started to empty it. He had just met up with one of Whyte's men to get the work for Jordyn. He was happy that she trusted him with her business, just as she did. He put the bricks of cocaine and the bricks of heroin on the table so that she could go through them and make sure that she had everything that she was supposed to have.

"Why do I feel like I'm the only one worried about Goldie? Is it me, or does it seem that no one else cares that he is gone? The police are half-ass searching, and his boys are halfway searching, too. All of this is a bunch of bullshit, I swear to God," Jordyn said as she noticed someone walking toward her front door on the monitor.

"Don't think like that. People just have different ways of handling things. No one is going to go as hard for your nigga like you, tho' you got to know that. Don't count everybody out. They are worried. I'm sure they are handling things differently because they feel differently about him than you do. I mean, no one can go kicking down doors and shooting up houses until he pops up," Chink said as he watched Jordyn looking at the security cameras that were displayed on the flat-screen television that was mounted on the wall.

"Why the hell can't they? Man, I'm telling you that is some bullshit. Now, what does this bitch want? I think that Goldie's mama is going to be a problem." Jordyn went to the front door and opened it. She then unlocked the burglar bars and stood there, looking at the lady. Goldie was the spitting image of her.

"Have you heard anything yet? They seem to be keeping stuff from me. I don't know why. I'm his mother," she said to Jordyn, who stood staring at her behind the door with a blank look.

"Oh, really? He didn't seem to think that you were his mother when he was out living on the streets, not knowing where his next meal was going to come from. Wayment, I got that backward; you didn't seem to think that he was your son when he was out living on the streets hungry."

"Goldie is a grown man. He could take care of himself. Look how far he made it. The streets only made him stronger. Plus, he was living with his baby mama and her mama. He was okay. Don't fall for that homeless shit. He just told you that to get in your panties. Look like it worked, he got that slick shit from his daddy. God rest his soul," Goldie's momma snapped back.

"You are wrong. I had known Goldie for a long time before our relationship. When I met him, he had only three shirts and one pair of pants. Goldie was living from pillar to post. He had been stopped dealing with Raquel's trifling ass. He told me she reminded him too much of someone he once knew. Tuh. But anyway, why do you keep coming to my doorstep? I'm sure the police have told you the same thing they told me. So you really don't need to come round these here parts, "Jordyn corrected her.

"We both know that he is dead. You need to face the truth. Let's give this some closure. We can have him a nice memorial service, where his friends and loved ones can be at peace, so I can go back where I came from." Goldie's mother said.

"And where exactly is this rock located that you slithered from? I'm not declaring him dead because he ain't dead. He didn't have a will, and if it ain't in my name already, I'm still over it because of the power of attorney. My advice for you is to just get started. I got your number; I will call you when he comes back home. Because he is coming back home. My man ain't dead, and even if he was, you would not get your hands on one red cent. I will donate it to charity first," Jordyn said as she stood at the door with her hands on her hips, her nostrils flared in anger.

"You can't donate anything to charity. He got kids and a baby mama," she hollered out.

"Right, and I will make sure that they are straight. Since Goldie has been missing, I haven't missed a beat. They still get the same amount of money every week that they were getting when their father was here with me. You haven't been worried about his kids. You haven't been worried about him. Please just get the hell on lady. I'm not the one that you want to go up against. You will not win. I promise you that." Jordyn's eyes narrowed into slits, and her voice dripped with venom.

Chink walked up behind her, he knew that Jordyn was filled with anger and he knew her next step was to open the door and beat the lady. She could give a damn who momma she was. He put his hand on her shoulder. He felt her exhale loudly. He said, "Don't worry about her. It takes more than one person to argue, leave her ass out there by herself."

"You moved on mighty quickly for you to be so worried about your MAN," Goldie's mom said sarcastically when she saw the interaction between Jordyn and Chink.

Jordyn locked the deadbolt on the burglar bars and slammed the big wooden door in his mother's face. She turned around and faced Chink. "We gotta snatch Head's daughter up. We get his daughter, I bet Goldie pops up."

"You know I will do whatever you want me to do. But have you thought this out? How do you know that Head has Goldie? We have no concrete evidence," Chink said as he looked at the pain in Jordyn's eyes.

"I feel it. The police stated that the camera at that intersection was not functioning, but the one at the previous intersection was. They caught a red Range Rover following closely behind Goldie's truck. Them niggas are Bloods. I guarantee you that all Heads' cars are red. I have already seen him in a red G-wagon and an Audi A8 at the kids' school. I'm telling you, I know what I know. And Dent is in on it. I bet you my last dollar in the bank, and that he is the reason why they got Goldie."

"Okay, well, are you straight? I'm about to head to the old neighborhood, throw some money around, and see what I can hear about Dent or Head. You know money talks. I gotta get in the field with this one. I'm not coming back until I have some type of info for you," Chink said as he headed toward the back where he had parked his car.

"Before you leave, put this work up. I think I'mma head home and be with my children. They always put a smile on my face. And you know what? That is the kicker, but don't you know what makes me think Dent is guilty? He has not called or tried to come and see the kids in God knows when. That is because of the guilt. He knows that I would be able to read him."

"Okay, call me when you make it in safely. I will be over later when I finish," Chink said as he put the bricks of dope back into the duffle bag and headed to put it in the safe room.

Jordyn ended up leaving out before Chink. She was so fed up and just didn't know where to turn. She got into the truck and buckled up her seatbelt. She just had to tell somebody about Goldie's mom and knew not to call Money for anything. "Call Whyte," she said into her Bluetooth as she turned off Griffin Street onto Lindsey Street.

Whyte answered, and they were busy talking; Jordyn never noticed the red Corvette following her down Bankhead Highway.

CHAPTER 14
Gotta find my way back

Chrissy walked into the house, hands loaded down with shopping bags. She was surprised to see her husband's car in the driveway. She had eaten while out with Pretty, so he would have to fend in the kitchen. She was exhausted. After her shopping spree with Mercedes, she had to go on one with Pretty cause he seemed to have an attitude the next day. Talking about somebody trying to steal his best friend.

Chrissy didn't want to tell Mercedes' business, so she let Pretty think what he may. Chrissy knew that she was still working on her good days, so she didn't believe that anyone needed to know about the cancer yet.

The aroma of food hit her suddenly, and although it smelled fantastic, it made her stomach queasy. She dropped her bags in the foyer and rushed to the restroom as the bile rose from her stomach. Chrissy emptied the contents of her stomach and was mad. She had enjoyed the seafood pasta from the Cheesecake Factory. She washed her face, rinsed her mouth, and left the bathroom. Whyte was standing in front of the restroom when she opened the door.

"I heard you coming in, and I wondered where you disappeared. Is everything alright?" Whyte said as he looked at his wife up and down with his eyebrow raised. His guilty conscience made him come home early and try to make things right with his wife. That was the thing about Chrissy; she didn't argue or fuss. She would just drift away. He couldn't risk losing her. He remembered when they first got together; she never had it out with her parents and sister. She started spending more time with him, eventually moving out and never looking back.

Chrissy was filled with panic; she felt like she was under a microscope as her husband's eyes roamed up and down her body. She wondered if he noticed a difference in her. Even though they had been sleeping with one another every night, that was all they had been doing.

"I, I, I mean me and Pretty ate at the Cheesecake Factory when we were out. I don't think it agreed with me," Chrissy stuttered nervously as she looked down at the floor instead of making eye contact with Whyte.

He reached out and grabbed her hand, but he felt her shaking. He grabbed her chin and lifted her head to look into her eyes. Something didn't feel right. Just as he was about to say something, his phone started to ring loudly. He thought that he had put it on silent. Whoever it was hung up and called again.

"You sure you are okay? I cooked one of your favorite meals. You want me to just put it up?" Whyte asked his wife as an uneasy feeling came over him when he locked eyes with her. His phone started to ring again.

"You can go ahead and take your call. It's probably business. Thank you for the meal, baby. I will put the food up and eat it later. I think the only thing I need to put on my stomach right now is some ginger ale." Chrissy broke away from her husband and left him in front of the restroom as she headed toward the kitchen. She heard him answer the phone, and she shook her head.

"I told you not to call me until tomorrow when I left you. So, what is the damn emergency? I'm in for the night. I will get with you tomorrow. No buts, tomorrow!" Whyte raised his voice as he ended the phone call abruptly. He turned around and saw his wife standing there, looking at him. Whyte couldn't read the look on her face. But he knew that she overheard his conversation. His phone started to ring again. He looked down at it and then looked up at his wife. This time it was Money. He answered the phone, hoping to hear some good news.

"What's up, bro? Yeah, I'm in for the night. Meet me at the warehouse tomorrow afternoon, and we can talk about business then. You know I don't talk on the phone. Okay, well, meet me at the barbershop around ten then. I got you. Holla at you tomorrow." This time, when Whyte looked up, he was standing downstairs alone. He took a deep breath and decided he wasn't ready to face his wife. He went into the game room and started shooting pool by himself.

Chrissy removed her clothes, turned around, and locked the bathroom door. She knew that the first call was from a woman because the volume on his phone was turned up. She shook her head as she looked at her naked body in the mirror. She touched her belly and swore that she noticed a baby bump. Chrissy wasn't ready for a baby, especially right now. Her husband was cheating and still selling drugs. The tears threaten to come from her eyes. She had to be strong. Maybe she just needed some time alone. She got into the shower, closed her eyes, and prayed as the tears fell freely. She didn't care because she needed the release. Some things she couldn't tell Mercedes, she couldn't tell Pretty, she didn't even tell Whyte.

She got out of the shower and dried off. This time, Chrissy didn't even look in the mirror; she just slipped on some sleep shorts and a t-shirt. She grabbed her iPad and put in her earbuds. The sounds of Bishop T. D. Jakes flooded her ears. He was one of her favorite pastors; she watched him online and had all his books. The topic of the sermon was 'Peace be still.' She got in bed, got under the covers, and listened to sermon after sermon until she fell asleep. Vowing before she closed her eyes that she would start back going to therapy. She needed to talk to someone before she imploded.

Whyte shot game after game before he finally came upstairs. He walked into their bedroom and noticed that his wife had fallen asleep. The smell of the expensive rose and sandalwood scented body wash flooded his senses. He stood over the bed, and he watched Chrissy sleep peacefully. He picked up the iPad, looked down, and saw that she was watching church online. Whyte started to feel bad; this let him know that his wife was hurting. He put the iPad on the nightstand and went into the bathroom to shower.

The guilt overwhelmed him. He had to do something to make it right, but he didn't know what to do. He had taken on more than he could handle. Everything was perfect when he took on the extra workload, and he had people to handle it. He didn't expect it to go this far when he started messing around with Imani. Now she was pregnant and harassing him, but he had moved on. He gave her ten thousand dollars and told her to handle her business, but here it was five months later, and now she was showing and threatening to tell his wife. He had to figure out a way to stop her. He ran his hands through his hair roughly and jumped into the shower. Whyte was in over his head, which significantly affected his wife.

He jumped in the shower and washed quickly. Instead of getting in bed with his wife, he entered the bedroom adjacent to the master suite. This was supposed to be his man cave. Whyte turned the television on ESPN and got into bed. So many thoughts were running through his head. He had many problems and was used to being the problem solver, but it seemed he didn't even have the answer. His name held weight, and where his name didn't matter, money did. But right now, it seemed like neither one of those could help alleviate the bullshit.

He tossed and turned, trying to get comfortable. Everybody always came to him with their problems, and he usually took his wife with him. Whyte knew he was in a fucked up situation because he couldn't go to his wife with some of this. He was a fixer and wanted to make everything right for everybody. That was what he was used to doing as a leader. But he couldn't cure Money's wife's cancer, he couldn't seem to find Goldie, and he couldn't make Dude act right with his wife. So, what he was going to do when he got up was focus on what he could make right. Starting with getting rid of Imani first. The news of her being pregnant would destroy his wife.

CHAPTER 16
Anything for you

Tameka sat at her desk typing the rest of the briefs needed for court for the next two days. She was tired; she had been trying to find out some info about her husband's friends, especially Whyte. Jonathan had been friends with him for years, and he'd always been a good guy. Still, after the party and the gift of the car, she felt like her husband's affiliation with him might be more than the average friendship.

She had recently started assisting another attorney and still had classes at night. Tameka patted herself on the back because even though she was tired, she wouldn't complain. She could say that she loved work, she loved school, and she definitely loved her family. All her hard work would pay off because, in a few years, Tameka would have a paralegal assisting her and a fully staffed office of her own.

Since Atlanta had become the entertainment mecca of the South, she knew she had made the right decision to enter entertainment law. Lord knows the entertainers here stayed in trouble. Her criminal justice degree and all the connections she had made with the judges and lawyers on all levels will be put to good use. She knew a lot of the cops because of her husband. She was destined to go straight to the top.

Tameka thought about the judge. She knew that if she was still involved with her, her name would be on the tongue of every rapper, singer, sports player, and actor who lived in the Metro Atlanta area. Without the judge, Tameka would have to let her hard work speak for itself. She got up to go to the printer to get her documents when her assistant came in with a large vase filled with red and white roses.

"Aww, you must have given Big Daddy some of that sloppy toppy that you told me about before you left home this morning," she said, laughing as she put the vase on the edge of Tameka's desk. She snatched the card from the bouquet while Tameka reached for it.

"Bitch, quit being nosey. How do you know it's from my husband? It could be from your fiancé. I mean, he did like me first," Tameka joked with her assistant, who was also her sorority sister, as she quickly snatched the envelope from her.

"My nigga ain't the flower-sending type of guy. Now, if that was a box from Chanel or Louis Vuitton, then I would have believed you. You know Ben doesn't know how to be low-key and sweet. He always gotta be loud and extravagant," she said as she walked toward the door.

"That is why you guys are perfect for one another. Tuh," Tameka said, laughing louder than she was expecting. She opened the card immediately. It was amazing because she was thinking about the judge and then received the flowers. Her first instinct was to call her and say thank you. She decided against it; she ripped the card into small pieces, put it in the trash, and walked down the hall to get all her documents.

"Hello, Mrs. Harper, how are you? Don't you look beautiful today?" the judge said to Tameka. She hoped she would run into her when she met with one of her colleagues.

"Thank you very much, your honor. You are looking nice, as well."

"I like your haircut. It is very attractive on you and complements your face."

Tameka felt uncomfortable under the judge's stare. She tried to walk around her to head into the copy and print room.

"Wow, that is all that you have to say? Did you get the flowers? How have you been doing? How is Londyn? I miss you so much. What can I do to make it up to you? Can we at least be friends?" The judge searched

Tameka's eyes to see some type of emotion. She didn't; her facial expression was blank, and her eyes were, too.

She answered the questions in rapid fire. "Yes, I received the flowers, thank you very much. I'm fine. Londyn is great and growing so much. Maybe one day, just not right now. I need to get my shit together." Tameka walked around the judge and headed into the copy and print room. None of her materials had been printed because there was no paper in the printer. She loaded the printer with paper, folded her arms, and waited for the hundreds of pages to print. She didn't have to turn around when she heard the footsteps come in behind her. She knew it was the judge. She smelled her scent.

The door slammed loudly, and Tameka didn't flinch; she kept her back turned and watched the paper shooting out of the printer like it was the most interesting thing in the world.

"You can't keep ignoring me and running from me. Don't you realize how much I love you? I would do anything for you. You are all that I have." The judge sniffed loudly. She was fighting back the tears.

"You didn't love me when that cop car smashed into me. You don't love me; you love how I make you feel. Please leave me alone before I say hurtful things I might regret." Tameka turned around, faced the judge, and was surprised to see that she was crying silently. She saw the pain in her eyes, and she walked around her and left the room.

"Tameka, you will need me; when you do, I will be right there. I'm not going to give up on you, even though you have given up on me," the judge said to her as she watched her walk back into her office. She looked around and saw several people in the office staring at her. She wiped her face and headed down the hall to her meeting.

Tameka sat back down at her desk and took a deep breath. She was not prepared for the encounter with the judge. Seeing her crying pulled at her heartstrings. An email alert appeared on her computer screen, and she opened it. It was from one of her sorority sisters who worked in the bureau. She requested the information on Whyte, Money, Dent, and Jordyn. She sent it to the printer and returned to get all her documents.

Walking down the hall, she thought about what the judge had said about her needing her. The fact that she felt she needed her to make it insulted her. Tameka knew she needed to work extra hard just to prove that she was right. Her cell phone vibrated in the holster on her hip; she removed it and answered it.

"I got the info, doll; I so appreciate it," she said immediately when she saw it was her soror.

"Awesome, I got one more tidbit of info that might be helpful. All those people were flagged except for the girl."

"Flagged? What does that mean? Speak none FBI language honey," Tameka said, laughing.

"That means they are already under investigation by another agent," she replied.

CHAPTER 17
Not doing Enough

J ordyn tossed and turned. Her body needed sleep, but her mind wouldn't let her get the rest. She needed to go ahead with the kidnapping plan because the longer that Goldie was gone, the greater the likelihood that they might hurt him.

She wished Pick had not moved to the West Coast with Julio to handle that branch of the business. Jordyn knew for sure that Pick would be able to find his brother and possibly talk some sense into him. Dent just didn't know he was making it worse for himself. With her anger building up against him, Jordyn didn't plan to have any mercy on him. This time, she was going to kill him, and Chink wasn't going to be able to stop her.

She got up, and surprisingly Chink wasn't there. She headed down the hall to check on the kids because she thought she heard some giggling. She pushed Peace's bedroom door open, and he and Joi sat in the middle of the bed playing Uno. Jordyn went inside smiling.

"Please tell me you guys haven't been up all night playing cards?" she said as she plopped down on the bed and peeked in both hands to see what they were holding.

"Nope, we were playing before we went to sleep, and started playing when we woke up. We really just practiced against each other; we got to get better because Destiny wins all the time," Joi said to her mother as she wrapped one of her arms around her neck and nuzzled her.

"The only reason she won is because she is a big kid," Peace said as he threw down a card.

"I'm the Uno master; who do you think taught Destiny how to play? Let's start over; this time, deal me in." Just being in their presence was like medicine. Jordyn was suddenly feeling better.

She didn't realize how much time had passed until her little sister walked into the bedroom and told her she needed to be dropped off for her piano lessons. "Uggggggggghhhhhh, whose idea was all these lessons?" Jordyn said as she got up from bed.

"We're gonna be ready for you, Destiny; we have been practicing," Peace said as he got off the bed and went and grabbed his aunt's hand.

"Yup, we are going to whoop your butt on the next game, so you better pray hard about it," Joi said, laughing.

Destiny laughed loudly at her niece and nephew. "It's gonna take more than staying up all night playing against each other to beat me. I'm the Uno master."

"Because mommy is the one who taught you!" Joi hollered.

"You guys put on your house shoes so you can ride with me to drop Destiny off. We can get Mickey D's on the way.

"I don't want Mickey D's. I want Waffle House," Joi said.

Jordyn looked at her daughter. "Girl, what do you know about the Waffle House?"

Destiny chimed in, "Chink buys us Waffle House just about every morning on the way to school when he takes us."

"I wish Goldie or Chink could've been our daddy," Peace said.

"Goldie is our new daddy," Joi followed up.

The dam broke, and Jordyn turned her back so they wouldn't see the tears that were coming out of her eyes. "Y'all go ahead and wash your face, brush your teeth, and put some shoes on so we can go get some Waffle House and drop your auntie off."

Jordyn sat on her bed, picked up the phone, and dialed it. "Bro, I'm losing it. Can y'all do something, anything? Just help me bring him home, please. I'm begging you."

"Sis, we are not doing enough. The search needs to be turned up several notches. What do you have in mind? Where should we start?" With Julio gone to the other side of the country and Money out of the game, Whyte needed Goldie here just as much. But hearing the pain and knowing that Jordyn was on the other end in tears solidified that he had to do whatever it was to bring Goldie home.

"I gotta plan. We just need to map it out," Jordyn said to Whyte, happy to hear he was with her.

"Okay, well, I will be out in a few. Meet me at the barbershop. We are going to figure out something."

* * *

Money slowly pulled into the barbershop parking lot. There was only one car there, and it belonged to the barber. He knew when he left home that he wanted to get a shave. He hopped out of his Corvette and put his pistol in his waistband before heading in. He didn't want to leave home because his wife had a bad day. Now, he could look at her and tell that she was sick. He hated it, hated that she was suffering like she was. If she hadn't told him that Dejah was coming over to spend the day with her and take care of her, Money would still be at home at his wife's side. She was his first priority, no matter what.

Ever since he told Biggs that he would give him the connect, he was back on his ass. Every time he turned around, he was pestering him to set up the meeting. Money was trying his best not to spaz out on his friend. He put his number on the call block after the last call. He would call him when he had some news. He planned on talking to Whyte about it today.

He walked in and sat down in the barber's chair. "Clean me up, homie. I have been doing it at home lately."

"I can tell." His barber laughed out loud as he threw the cape on and started to prepare his face for the straight razor.

"You're booked up, man. I don't have time to just chill in the barbershop anymore. I'm constantly on the go," Money told the only barber he had been coming to for the last ten years.

"I understand, at least you are not letting anybody else fuck you up.

I hate when my regulars go to another barber and then come in here begging me to fix the fuck ups. But anyway, how is the wife and the princess? I saw her the last time I was picking up my kids from the skating rink. I hope you got your shotgun loaded because I keep mine in the back of the cab of the pickup. They are growing up so fast. I ain't ready for this man," he said as he lathered Money's face and head.

"I know you aren't. You were so wild back then, and you had all the girls. I hope you are praying that God doesn't punish you," Money said, laughing at his friend.

"When we had our second daughter, I looked to the sky and told him that I knew this was punishment for my wild days when I dragged those girls through these west side streets."

"Speaking of back in the day, have you seen Biggs yet?" Money said as he looked up at Whyte and Jordyn, who walked in the door.

"Somebody told me he was out, but I didn't believe them. Especially since you had not said anything to me about him. How long has he been free? I know he knows where I'm at; I wonder why dat nigga ain't come and hollered at me?"

"Who y'all talking bout?" Whyte said as he sat in the barber chair and started swinging in semi-circles.

"Biggs is out," Money said to Whyte in a low tone.

"Your old running partner? I remember hearing y'all talk about him. He was before my time, though. By the time I hit Atlanta, he was well into his sentence."

"How in the hell did that nigga get out? I thought he had life plus some," Jordyn said as she sat in her usual seat.

He was happy that Jordyn spoke. It showed that she wasn't mad at him anymore. Money had not even thought about all the time that Biggs got when he was sentenced. Now, the wheels started turning in his head. He thought to himself. *How did that nigga get out so early?* Money never asked, and Biggs never told.

"He was probably like my little cousin. That nigga was in there taking every class and participating in every workshop or rehabilitation class that he could. And when he went up for parole, they would let him come home if no one disputed it." The barber volunteered as he waved the razor back and forth across Money's head.

"They need to let some of the real niggas go anyway. Man, the streets are fucked up out here without them," Whyte said.

"Speaking of real niggas, can we talk about mine? All this Money and power that we got in this city, you mean to tell me that we can't put our feet on a few necks to squeeze these niggas out? Come on now, you can't be for real. Y'all have let all the young niggas and new niggas come in and take over. I need y'all's help, but I will do it myself if I have to. But I'm telling you right now, it will not be pretty. I'm shooting first and asking questions later. No ifs, ands, or buts about it." The dark circles were a sharp contrast against Jordyn's light skin. She was definitely not getting any rest.

"I told you a few weeks ago that you can not just go in guns blazing. You need to think this out," Money said, knowing that Jordyn would snap off on him. He hoped that Whyte would jump in and talk some sense into her.

"My nigga has been missing for well over a month. The police ain't doing shit, we ain't doing shit. He is just somewhere out there, whether he is dead or alive. Goldie needs to be found. Immediately!" You could hear the frustration in her voice.

"But, but," Money spoke before Jordyn cut him off.

"Ain't any buts in this shit. Don't you wake up to your wife every morning? Right, well, you can't speak on what the fuck I'm going through. I just thought you would have been in the trenches getting dirty digging to find your so-called lil' bro." Tears fell down her face, and her voice started to shake when talking to Money. It hurt her to her core because she thought that even if they weren't riding with Goldie, they would be out looking for him just because he was her man and she was their family.

"Calm down, Jay. We will have a plan in place by the end of the day, and it will be implemented before the sun goes down. Puncho is meeting up with me later on; just stay with me, and you can talk to him," Whyte said. Inside, he was hurting for Jordyn. He was hurting because he didn't want Goldie to think that he hadn't tried his best to bring him home safe or get the niggas who did that to him.

The barber laid the hot towel on Money's face, and he walked to the back of the shop. He took this opportunity to bring up the work. "Aye, bro, I need to get four of them things from you A.S.A.P." Money looked over, and Jordyn and Whyte's eyes had doubled in size.

"Nigga, what are you going to do with four bricks? I thought you were finished. You trying to ease your way back in?" Whyte asked, confused because four bricks of cocaine were lightweight compared to what Money used to push.

"Nawl, I'm just trying to look out for Biggs. He got some out-of-town contacts he met and is trying to get straight."

"You vouch for him? I know he is your partner, but I don't know him. I don't fuck with strangers. That is one of the reasons why I have lasted this long in the game." Whyte wanted the best for his buddy, but he was halfway wishing that Money was about to tell him that he wanted to get back in the game. He needed some help. Even though Jordyn was moving her usual units, Whyte had more than three times that sitting, waiting to be moved. He didn't want to put more pressure on her since she was going through this with Goldie.

"Yeah, you can put my face on it. Biggs got the cash for two, and I'm getting the other two for him. His money is good, and he is a hard worker. He's going to need more when these are all gone. I need to introduce him to you so I won't have to be the middle man," Money said happily that he had gotten that out of the way.

"Yeah, whatever. I gotcha," Whyte said as he looked down at his vibrating phone. He hoped it would be his wife because he had left without saying anything. But it wasn't, it was Imani. She was a pest; this was the first of what he knew would be many more phone calls throughout the day. He went ahead and answered it as he stepped outside the barbershop to talk in private.

"Hey, baby, did you sleep well? I was calling to see if you're still attending my appointment today. I'm going to have my first 3-D ultrasound," Imani said sweetly.

Whyte exhaled loudly, "No, Imani, I'm not going to this or any other appointments. How many times do I have to tell you that you are on your own on this one? I gave you the money to take care of the business, and you didn't. This is not my child, it is your child."

"You are just saying that now. Just wait, you are going to love her. I already know that she is going to look just like you. This is our blessing;

I wasn't going to kill our blessing," Imani said, trying to convince Whyte about the unborn child.

"You think it's a blessing because you will be getting money from me forever. I don't want you or that baby. Just leave me the hell alone." Whyte hung up the phone just as Jordyn was coming out of the barbershop.

"I'm ready to go when you are, bro."

"Okay, let me tell Money we're headed to the warehouse." He stuck his head inside the door and relayed the info to Money, standing up and paying the barber.

"Okay, I'm right behind y'all," Money said as he gave the barber some dap and headed out.

"Be careful, my brother; something doesn't feel right," the barber told him.

"There you go with that. I'm always careful. Go throw a chicken for me then," Money said, laughing as the door closed.

CHAPTER 10
Right under my nose

C haney slipped on the leggings and t-shirt her mother had bought her to wear home slowly. She laughed out loud to nothing in particular. Chaney couldn't wait to see the look on her husband's face when she turned the key and opened the door at home. But knowing Dude, he probably had gotten the locks changed, and if he did, she was going to call the police, because that was still her residence.

"Why do you have to go back there? You can just come home with me. Nobody is there but me," her mother said as if she was inside her head.

"That is my home. I'm going to be alright, Momma. You don't have to worry about me. I know how to handle my husband," Chaney said as she slipped on her Gucci flip-flops.

"Yeah, right. Look at what handling your husband has got you. How about I just stay here for a month or two? Just to make sure that you are good, help you get around, take you back and forth to therapy or whatever you need." Her mother did not want to leave her daughter alone with that monster in this big city.

"Momma, I'm not handicapped; I can take care of myself. Your life is in Augusta. You don't need to put your stuff on hold for me. Now quit looking so sad, and let's break out of this joint." Chaney put her arm inside her mother's, and they headed downstairs to where the car service was waiting. She had all of her balloons, cards, and flowers carried over to Hughes Spalding Children's Hospital across the street. As Chaney thought about the flowers, she stopped, pulled out her cell phone from her purse, and powered it on. She called Whyte to ask him to meet them at the house, just to be on the safe side. He didn't answer.

She was so thankful for him. He had been visiting her every day, bringing magazines, fresh flowers, and whatever she wanted to eat. Initially, she was skeptical when he told her he hadn't heard from Dude, but then she started to believe him. It was like her husband had disappeared off the face of the earth. Chaney was just going to enjoy peace of mind and hope that he would stay wherever he was.

They got off the elevator, and the lobby was crowded with people. The sun was shining and bright, and she could see that the outside of the hospital was just as crowded. Chaney wished that she had some sunglasses with her. A group of young boys walked past them, talking loudly and cursing. Her mother held on to her tightly.

"These young boys are so disrespectful. They don't even care about being in the presence of their elders. I don't see why you love being in the big city. Isn't that the detective that came to see you when you first were admitted?" she asked as she pointed to the tall, older black man walking in their direction.

Chaney squinted her eyes to block the sun and saw it was the detective. She smiled at him, waved, and continued heading toward the door.

"Mrs. Smith, it's good to see you are up and around. I was on my way to see you. I'm happy that I caught you. We have located your husband. I'm actually on my way to interview him regarding the accident you were involved in." The detective looked at Chaney closely to see her reaction. Ever since he first met this young lady, he just couldn't put two and two together. The story she told him made no sense, but it never changed.

"Well, there goes your theory that he was dead in the woods, and that is why he hasn't come to the rescue. I told you from the jump that his no-good ass left you there to die, but you didn't want to believe me." Chaney's mother's tone was so harsh.

Her eyes watered; the truth always hurt. She sniffled loudly and cleared her throat. "Where did you find my husband?" Chaney asked

"Actually, he is here. He was brought in with severe internal injuries. I received the call earlier because I put him on the missing list. If he was hospitalized or locked up, a hit would come across my desk," the officer said.

"When was he admitted?" she asked, but she already knew the truth.

"He came in a few days ago...."

Chaney didn't need to hear any more; she had been in the hospital for weeks. She silently wished that he would've died; that way, she would get everything that she earned without him putting up a fight.

The detective stood there staring at the beautiful young lady; her mother was also stunning. He wondered if she was single. He would find out that he had both of their phone numbers. He knew he would have to call them after the interview with the husband.

* * *

Chelsea was exhausted; she had been at Dude's bedside ever since he had been admitted to the hospital. Whenever she got ready to leave, he would beg her to stay, and she did. Chelsea hated Grady and wanted Dude to be transferred to Emory after he was taken off the oxygen machine. There was just something about it; she hated going downstairs to the cafeteria and snack area because it was always so crowded with all kinds of people.

The pain had been too much for him earlier, so they had given him morphine. Now that he seemed to be in a deep sleep, she decided she was going to go home and clean herself and take a nap in her own bed. Chelsea got up quietly and left the room.

As soon as the doctor saw the young lady getting on the elevator, he headed toward his patient's room. He had some things that he needed to discuss with him in private. He walked into the room and opened the blinds. He checked the patient's oxygen level. It had improved tremendously since yesterday afternoon when he last checked it. The fact that he had survived so long without medical attention was a blessing. Coping with a punctured lung or a ruptured spleen on just pain medication was damn near unbelievable, but with both, I still had the doctor in shock.

"Mr. Smith, Mr. Smith," he said as he lightly shook the patient's shoulder.

Dude thought that he was dreaming. He opened his eyes slowly, and the doctor stood at his bedside. He reached up and pulled the oxygen mask down off his face.

"Yes?"

"How are you feeling? Your oxygen levels are a lot higher today. I need to talk to you about what I learned after reviewing your tests." The older doctor sat down in the chair that was on the side of the bed.

"I feel a lot better, doctor. You know how women are; they think they can fix everything," Dude replied as he tried to adjust himself in the bed.

"Yes, I agree my wife is the same. I got some bad news. Your spleen is ruptured, and that is why you were bleeding internally. You also punctured your left lung. You are stabilized, but I'm going to send you for another CT scan. I do not operate unless it is absolutely necessary. But with your condition, I really do not want to go inside because I'm not sure how your body is going to respond to even more trauma. How long have you been H.I.V. positive, and what medications are you currently taking?" the doctor asked Dude in a somber tone.

There was a light tapping at the door, and before Dude could respond, an older, tall gentleman opened the door and peeped inside. "Hello, I'm Detective James Griffin. Are you Antonio Smith? I have a few questions for you."

CHAPTER 19
No New Niggas Allowed

Jordyn exited the truck with Whyte and followed him into the warehouse. The silence was killing her. She could tell that he had a lot on his mind. She just hoped that one of those things was how to bring Goldie home. She had tried to avoid bothering everyone and staying out of their way, so they could handle things, but it seemed they were not handling anything.

"How is the wifey doing?

"She is good, busy as always. Chrissy's gonna take over the world one day," Whyte said, unlocking the heavy metal door. He quickly keyed in the code on the keypad and looked around for Puncho; he saw his car parked outside.

"That's my kind of girl right there, then. She seemed so cool when I met her at the grand opening party. And her best friend, Pretty, is hilarious. He makes you like him."

"Yup, that is Pretty for you. I thank God for him. I just don't let him know. He is a lifesaver," Whyte said just as he saw Puncho coming out of the restroom.

"What's up, you guys? I hope we're in and out as quickly as we were the other day, because I need to take Londyn to get new sneakers that dropped this morning.

"Boy, I got a sneaker plug. I can get my guy to deliver whatever is exclusive to your front door. You will never have to set foot in a shoe store again. I met him through Goldie. I can hit him up when we finish handling this business," Whyte said as he headed to the loading area.

"I definitely need his info. I get tired of waking up at the crack of dawn every Saturday to get those damn Jordans. Dent used to do it, and then Goldie got them, but I didn't know he had a plug. I was just happy that he was making it happen. Damn, I miss my man," Jordyn said somberly.

"Sis, we all miss him," Puncho said as he got the crowbar and opened one of the crates. He took out the block of Styrofoam and fanned away the coffee beans. Underneath were neatly wrapped blocks of cocaine stacked on top of one another.

"I already got so much of this shit. But as long as Ponchees sends it to us, I might as well get it. Sis, you need to take about twenty with you," Whyte said as he got the crowbar and opened the other wooden crate.

There was loud banging at the door. "That probably is Money," Jordyn said as she headed to open the front door.

Whyte squinted his eyes, looked at the flat screen on the wall, and saw it was Money. "Yeah, that's him. He wants four bricks; I need that nigga to get like ten. I'm gonna have to get out here in the trenches and get me a trap house. I got too much work to get off of and not enough niggas that I trust to get rid of it."

"You can't start back trapping. You don't know the street-level people. What about those young niggas that were working for Goldie? Bring them on; I know they would be willing to work for you. They look up to you already," Puncho said; the last thing he needed to do was to cover for Whyte's ass more than he already was doing. He didn't plan on touching the dope when he signed up to join the organization. Now, here, he was in charge of the incoming shipments.

"Who do you think I have moving my shit? Those are my men. I'll take ten off your hands, even though my head isn't concentrating on hustling. I'm thankful that I got Chink and my brother handling the heavy side of my business. I will get rid of it. I think I still have three or four left from the last time, and that is why I haven't re-upped yet," Jordyn said as she sat on a folding chair. When she opened the door and rushed back to the guys, she didn't notice that Money had someone with him.

"You just be stretching the hell out of the dope, that is why you still got some. I don't know what you are doing. You put your cut on it, but your customers still loves it. This is my bro Biggs. Biggs, this is my bro, Puncho, Whyte, and my sis Jordyn," Money said, observing the odd look on everyone's face.

"What's up, my niggas? Hey, pretty lady. Bro talks about y'all all the time. It's nice to be able to meet you," Biggs said, noticing how they looked at one another.

"Well, the first time I heard about you was this morning. But it's nice to meet you." Jordyn didn't like the way he was looking at her.

Puncho couldn't take his eyes off of him. The hair on the back of his neck was standing up. Money was violating majorly. Rule number 1, don't trust no new niggas.

"Aye, let me call Julio and tell him everything is intact. I let that slip my mind. He pulled out his cell phone and walked away.

Whyte looked down at his bare arms and wondered where the chill bumps had come from. He looked up, and Biggs stared at him and smiled like the Joker.

"Aye, tell that nigga that he could answer the phone for me when I call," Money hollered at Puncho. He headed toward the wooden crate and looked in.

"You miss it, don't you?" Whyte asked as he watched Money pick up the brick of cocaine out of the crate.

"Nope, not really. Hustling is in me, but I can hustle anything, not just dope. You get a thrill out of the street shit. How many shipments are you getting in a week?" Money asked as he put the dope back.

"Let me just put it like that, this. I'm the dope man's, dope man," Whyte said, laughing at himself.

"Yup, bro, you are the only one doing it on this level round here, so even when a nigga thinks he ain't fucking with you, he is still fucking with you," Jordyn said.

Puncho joined them after the phone call, and he noticed how Money's friend's eyes were wandering all over the place taking everything in. He could only get back in here if he had a tank. This place was solid.

"Money, go ahead and get six, so you can get some of this shit off of my hands. I damn sure miss you in the field. You would retire right before we expanded."

He looked at Biggs, who was smiling like a Cheshire cat. "You think that you can handle six?"

"Hell yeah, I could probably get rid of ten of them thangs. I got niggas that are waiting on me to get my hands on the work, I'm telling you. I sure 'preciate you turning me on to the plug, I'mma be one of his best customers and it ain't gonna mess with nothing you already got going on. Most of my plays are coming from my folks out of town," Biggs said as he eyed the crate full of cocaine greedily.

"You don't have to rush. Take your time, bro; you need to get your feet wet. How many times am I going to have to tell you that shit has changed out here?" Money said.

"I know, I know. I'm listening, bro."

Suddenly, it seemed like time stopped when the loud boom seemed to shake part of the warehouse. Everyone immediately hit the floor. Smoke was everywhere, and so were the police, dressed in tactical gear, helmets, and masks.

Puncho looked up from where he was lying and saw the letters on the back of the bulletproof vest and felt like his world had officially come to an end.

CHAPTER 20
Plotting On The Low

D ent paced the floor back and forth nervously. He held his tongue because he really wanted to spaz out. He couldn't believe that his baby mama had gotten locked up, and by the Feds at that. What the fuck were these niggas thinking? He knew they wanted his old crew out of the way, but he didn't think they'd go this far. He didn't know what he had gotten himself into. This wasn't what he bargained for.

"Shiiiiiiiiiiiit!" He hit the wall hard with his fist.

Head sat there and continued to play the PlayStation. When he heard Dent's fist crash into the wall, he looked up with one eyebrow raised. He was quite amused at the whole situation. He knew Dent didn't have it in him to say anything out of pocket to him. It was not out of respect, but out of fear. Dent was a pussy nigga no matter what team he was on.

Who was in the warehouse? Well, it doesn't matter as long as they've got the key players. No wonder you're always sitting in silence. You're plotting on the low. I swear you gotta be the smartest nigga I know. Nobody else could have come up with a plan like that. Hell, I was thinking we needed to wet all of 'em up to get 'em off the streets. This is perfect because we don't have any blood on our hands, or any fingers pointing our way," Turtle said to Head. He wasn't paying attention to Dent throwing the hissy fit. He had gotten used to Dent's bitch-like ways because he spent the most time with him alone.

"Yup, now we just need him to handle his issue with ol' boy in the back, and the whole crew will be wiped out." Head shot Dent a side eye.

Dent was just about to leave the house before he got the news about Jordyn. He was tired of babysitting Goldie, tired of taking low blows from Head, and tired of not making any money. His situation wasn't better; in fact, it seemed worse to him.

"So I see that I'm going to have to off this nigga before you put any real work in my hand. I'm not used to handling this small amount," Dent said to no one in general. He was trying his best not to sound like he had an attitude.

"From what I've heard, you ain't used to handling any work. You're going to have to do something around here to man up. Because this shit right here ain't cutting it. I see why your folks treated you like they did. Lil' buddy, you're not ready to bark with the big dogs on a daily basis. Or maybe all you do is bark, cause you damn sho' ain't biting."

Dent bit down on his bottom lip so hard that it felt like he drew blood. He took a deep breath. He was so close to the edge that he didn't need to be pushed. "You won't even give me a chance. Just put the shit in my hands and I guarantee you that I will get off of it. I promise I will bring you back your money on time or before time, not a dollar short. Folks in the streets fuck with me. Just let me prove myself, big homie."

He hated to see a man beg, and it sounded like Dent was pleading. "I don't care how much money you see. I don't care how much dope you see. I can't afford to take any losses. I don't take losses. I can't count how many niggas are in the cemetery because they played with my money."

"I ain't going to play with it. You got my word. I just appreciate you believing me enough to get me from around them snake ass niggas and put me in a position to make some real money and finally be the boss type of nigga that I suppose to be." Dent was excited, and it seemed like the anger he was just displaying was out the window.

"Go get this nigga a nine. He gets rid of that, then give him a brick," he instructed Turtle before turning to Dent.

"Don't talk to me about no work no more. Go to Turtle for everything from now on. Go with him down the street to get the work. I will sit right here until y'all get back. Then I'm heading out. "

Turtle's eyes got big when he heard Head tell Dent to go with him to the stash house. He didn't say anything because he knew not to question Head's words. But he was wondering what the hell he had up his sleeve. Head never did anything without looking at the bigger picture.

Onc thing Head knew for sure was that if you give anybody enough rope, they would hang themselves. So he was issuing out rope to this nigga because he had gotten enough information from him to complete his mission. It was time to cut ties with the Dent situation because he wasn't built to be part of this team. He wanted some work, so he was going to give him some work.

Head walked down the hall to the restroom, and he heard bumping around in the room where Goldie was being held. Instead of going into the restroom, Head took out his keys and unlocked the two-deadbolt locks that held the metal and wooden door. This room used to be the stash room, but he moved the work to another spot when Goldie was kidnapped. When he opened the door, Goldie was sitting up on the bed. This was the first time he had seen him in person since the night in the club.

Goldie's eyes were sunk in his head, and his cheeks looked hollow. His complexion looked dull, and he had lost a lot of weight. He looked like he wasn't well, but he didn't look like he would be dying within the next few days. Head had to admit even to himself that Shorty was a fighter.

After seeing how Dent was and how Raquel moved, he felt sorry for Goldie. He got caught up with the wrong folks. Right now, instead of being held captive in a trap house, he would be in federal holding. Either way it goes, the youngster wouldn't be on the streets.

"You finally show your face. I knew you were behind this anyway. Dat nigga Dent doesn't have enough sense to pull shit like this off. Without Jordyn, he doesn't have a pot to piss in or a window to throw it out. You'll see soon enough that you have the wrong person on your team. If a nigga will stab his best friend in the back who has clothed him, fed him, bailed him out of jail, and kept niggas off his ass for almost twenty years. What do you think he'll do to some niggas he's known for six months? I might be dead when you realize it, but just remember, I told you first." Goldie was still weak, but he was feeling stronger than he had since he had been held captive.

The wheels were turning in his head before he came into the room with Goldie. Dent wasn't an asset to anyone; all he was good for was the information about Whyte's crew. "If he was so bad, why did ya man, Whyte, keep him around for so long?"

Goldie looked Head in the eyes. He often wondered that himself over the years since he had been in the organization. "They've been friends for years. When you don't have family, your friends become your family. Dent's face card is good in all the hoods, so he can go anywhere and get information. He is flashy, so the women like that. But he's not the nigga he says he is. Jordyn is that nigga. But only people on the inside know that. She hustles all of the work, stays in the trap from sun-up to sundown. Take care of her kids and her mom's kids. He told you a lot of shit, but he didn't tell you that his baby momma is harder than most niggas. She is the reason why he got everything he got, right down to the draws on his ass. That is why the nigga is mad at me. I didn't take his girl; she was tired of being gay fucking with his bitch ass."

Head took off his baseball cap and started to scratch his bald, tattooed head. Now everything was making sense. Head was thinking that Whyte was paying Dent to be the cheerleader. But in actuality, his baby momma was the one taking care of him. That is why he really hated Goldie, not because he took his bitch. He took his way of life. Jordyn was the breadwinner.

"Damn, I knew she was getting to a lil' bread, but she really wasn't on my radar like that. No wonder the feds snatched her up, too."

"Feds! Snatched who up?" Goldie yelled, almost leaping off the bed.

Head stood back. He was startled at Goldie's reaction.

"I hope that fuck nigga gon' see bout his kids. Man, I can't believe this shit. You did this? All this muthafucking money in this city and you setting folks up to get busted? Is this how they do it on the West Coast?

I'm a Grady baby, and if I want your spot, I don't knock you off or get you busted. I just offer something better. How do you think I took that nigga's girl? I offered something better. Y'all west coast niggas got the game fucked all the way up," Goldie said. He couldn't hide the fact that he was worried about his family. They were all he had and the only hope he had of getting saved.

Gut Feelings

Tameka wanted to stay in bed but knew she had to go to work. She had only been sleep two hours before her alarm clock sounded. She had been up trying to study for an exam that she had to take in class tonight after work. School was the last thing on her mind, and it seemed her life was crashing around her. She still put on a brave face every day and went to work and school despite her husband's face being plastered all over the news for the last week.

The media was making it seem like he was Day-Day of the Diablos. She really wanted to reach out to the judge to see if there was anything that she could do about it, but she decided against it. She felt that it was best if she just let sleeping dogs lie.

Tameka rolled out of bed and headed to the bathroom. She heard her son, Londyn, moving around. He had been so distant since Jonathan had been locked up. She wanted to hide it from him. She didn't tell him the first night. But he came home with his shirt ripped the next day because he had gotten into a fight with one of the kids who called his dad a dirty cop.

Her gut never led her wrong. She had been feeling odd ever since the night of the grand opening party of Luxurious. She missed something while with her husband and his friends that night. It was like something unspoken there, and she was left out.

Tameka knew that Whyte was one of her husband's best friends, but he had just bought him a sports car that cost over fifty thousand dollars. Not letting all the investigative skills she had learned in school go to waste, she watched her husband's every move. Because Tameka knew for a fact that big gifts like those came at a price, no matter what was said. She was a living witness.

When she exited her master bathroom, she heard the music blaring from the den. This could be a sign that her son had awakened in good spirits. Tameka put a smile on her face and headed in that direction. She didn't want him to know that she had been crying herself to sleep every night since her husband had been incarcerated.

Londyn was in the kitchen at the stove, flipping pancakes. He had a carton of eggs, shredded cheese, and a pack of turkey bacon on the counter. "I know you've got a long day ahead, so I wanted to send you off like you do me when I have a test."

Her heart smiled, and the tears started to fall. She remembered the cooking lessons that Puncho used to give Londyn. He was so good to both of them and deserved to be home with his family. He was not the monster that the media portrayed him to be. Tameka got the apple juice out of the refrigerator for Londyn and started the Keurig for coffee for herself.

"I would like some coffee, too, mommy," Londyn said as he laid strips of bacon in a baking dish and placed them in the oven.

"Coffee, boy, you don't need any coffee. You will be bouncing off the walls in school. You will be having a glass of apple juice. I know your daddy wouldn't give you any coffee first thing in the morning," she said to him.

"Daddy and I always stop at Starbucks on the way to school. What are you talking bout? The coffee helps me, but I ain't going to school today. I'm suspended."

Tameka exhaled loudly. She didn't even want to ask what he was suspended for because she knew he was probably defending himself. "For how long?"

"Five days, but I don't want to go back. Can I just do homeschool?

Things are not going to change in five days. Everywhere I turn, somebody has something to say. Even the principal said something to me. She didn't mean any harm, but I don't want to hear it. I wish we could just move away. I'm tired of hearing about it already."

"Don't you listen to anything anyone says about your father. That is your father, and you know him best. Don't let anyone in the street tell you about his worst. Now, I will research getting you into a homeschool program. Put my breakfast into a to-go container. Keep your cell phone and the home phone right here with you, and I will be FaceTiming you during the day to ensure you are in place. Londyn, do not leave this house for nothing. Everything that you need is right here."

"I'm not going anywhere, mommy. I have enough schoolwork to last me until next year. They loaded me down like all the assignments were a punishment. I like doing my homework and will continue to make you and Daddy very proud. This is not a stop sign, more like a speed breaker." Londyn turned around and put food into a plastic container for his mother to take to work.

Tameka was in shock at the maturity that her son displayed. She walked up behind him, wrapped her arms around him tightly, and kissed his head. "I held us down for ten years before your dad came into the picture. I got us now, and I don't care if I have to cross oceans to bring your father home, as an innocent man."

CHAPTER 22
All Cried Out

Chrissy was tired of crying. She walked back and forth from her closet to her bed as she tried to clean up the mess that the police had left when they came into her house and tore it to pieces looking for God knows what. They had confiscated a safe, two laptops, and three guns. There was nothing inside her residence that was illegal. They had to know that her husband had not made it this long in the game without thinking about every possible scenario. Her mind instantly went to Mercedes. They had started to form a beautiful friendship. She had to check on her to make sure that she was okay.

Her phone started to ring, and it was like they were on the same wavelength. A picture of Mercedes and Money popped up on her phone. "Are you okay? The feds just left my condo. They turned it upside down. They didn't find anything. I just wish my baby weren't at home. I didn't want her to see that. Bad enough they had them splattered on the news this morning like they were some damn serial killers."

"Awww man, Heavyn was there when they came? I'm sorry bout that, Mercedes. What did she say?" Chrissy sat down on her bed and wiped her face as she talked to Mercedes.

"She was just quiet. She sat there with her head down in the corner.

This is too much for her. We just told her the other day about the cancer. I couldn't hide that anymore. All my hair has fallen out, I'm constantly vomiting, and I'm lying around on the days after chemo. She is not a dummy. I wouldn't be surprised if she didn't know what was going on already, but just didn't say anything."

Chrissy thought to herself that was one of the main reasons why she didn't want to have kids while Whyte was still in the streets. She didn't want her children to have to go through this type of shit because of her husband's greed. They were already wealthy.

"I'm here if you need me. I need to find out what is going on with Jordyn's kids. If she is locked up and Goldie is missing, who do they have? I know she's in there, going crazy. I need to make sure they are being taken care of so that DFACS can't get involved."

"I'm sure that her brother and her best friend are making sure that they are fine." As soon as Mercedes said that, it made her thankful for Dejah. She was the closest thing to a sibling that she had.

"You know I am a mother hen without the children. I just have to make sure that everyone is good. I wonder if they are going to close down the club. We need to get together and go over there and see what is going on," Chrissy replied. People always spoke of her nurturing spirit. She would make a good mother one day.

"Speaking of everyone, oh, my God. Have you seen how they are doing, Puncho? The media is ripping him a new asshole. The mayor held a press conference about it. Girl, we need to reach out to his wife and son. I hope she is alright. This can't be good for her; she is in the law profession. I'm not sure what she does, but I know she is constantly in and out of court." Mercedes was hoping that things would get better before they got worse.

"I'm about to get on my knees before I make these calls and lift everyone up in prayer. Hopefully, they will let us call them soon so we will know what is going on. You can't believe everything that the media tells you."

"Honey, the media are the last people that I believe. They have stories so misconstrued. I do not believe one word. I need everything from my husband's mouth. My baby and I are about to get on our knees, as well. I will call you if I hear something, and you do the same. I will talk to you later, girl."

Chrissy ended the call, got on her knees on the side of her bed, and closed her eyes. Her husband was a strong man, and he could handle himself better than most. But he also had never been in any trouble with the law in his life.

"Heavenly Father, please keep my husband safe and sound. Keep him strong in his resolve, his mind, body, and his strength. Keep him true to his word and even truer to his code, and please bring him home safe. Please watch over all the families of everyone involved."

"Amen!" Pretty said, finishing up the prayer as he walked into Chrissy's bedroom and witnessed her on the floor praying. He knew that Whyte meant the world to her, and she wouldn't be right with him not home.

"Do you have to walk so lightly? You are quieter than a cat. I didn't even hear the door chime when you came in. But then again, they messed up so much shit when they broke the door, they might have fucked up the alarm and chime. Speaking of which, I need to call the repairmen to fix that door. I ain't going to lie, I don't even want to stay here."

"Girl, you can come over to my house, it will be like a big slumber party." Pretty didn't know what to say to make things better, but knew that sometimes that just being there was enough.

"I haven't even been to sleep. I don't know if I am going or coming. Help me clean up some of this mess. I'm about to make a few calls." Chrissy picked up her cellphone and walked out of her bedroom as Pretty started to put the drawers back in the chest.

And It Don't Stop

Jordyn lay on her back with her hands behind her head and stared at the ceiling. This was her first time alone since she got locked up. They came and picked up her roommate this morning for court. She was still in shock; she couldn't believe that they had locked her up; hell, they had locked all of them up. When it rains, it pours. She sat in silence by herself. She knew that she needed to shake the depression that hung over her like a rain cloud. Everything went from damn near perfect to the worst in the blink of an eye. This could not be her life. She felt so overwhelmed and didn't know what to do. Whenever she didn't know what to do, she would pray. She hopped her petite frame off the top bunk and knelt in prayer.

"Adams, you got a visitor," the correction officer's voice filled her cell through the intercom system.

She had refused two other visits last week but knew she had to talk to whoever came to see her. She needed to see what was going on in the outside world. Jordyn drew the crucifix across her chest even though she had not started to pray. She knew she couldn't continue to pout; she had three children who needed her to be strong.

As she pushed the loose hairs back up into the messy bun on her head, the steel door opened slowly. The correction officer was standing there with the shackles and handcuffs in her hand, ready to take her to visitation right down the hall.

"Turn around, please, ma'am," she said politely.

Jordyn couldn't understand why she had to be shackled like a mass murderer when all she was doing was going right down the hall. Her eyes got big, and then she exhaled loudly and turned around so she could be handcuffed and her feet could be shackled. When the officer kneeled and secured her legs together, the tears started to fall. She knew she didn't need to be on her knees for God to hear her prayers. She began to pray silently, hoping to soon get home to her children safe and sound, and that Goldie would be there waiting for her.

Just the thought of Goldie made even more tears fall from her eyes. The invisible faucet had been turned on, and with her hands in the cuffs, she couldn't even wipe her eyes as she shuffled down the hall to the small room where she would talk to whoever came to visit her on a phone receiver behind two inches of thick plexiglass.

The officer opened the door after removing the handcuffs, and sitting on the other side of the glass was Chink. He sat on the small metal bench, twiddling his thumbs. His eyes lit up when he saw Jordyn walk in and sit down on an identical bench. She raised her small palm and touched the glass after wiping her tears. She had never been so happy to see another human being.

Chink reached up and put his palm on the cold plexiglass. She looked exhausted. The circles were so dark around her eyes that it looked like she had two black eyes because of her light complexion. The navy blue prison jumpsuit swallowed up her tiny body, and her hair was unkempt, but she was still his Jay. He picked up the receiver and motioned through the glass for her to do the same.

"What's up, Shorty? I'm happy that you decided to finally let me see you. I have been so worried. What happened to you? You forgot how to use the phone? I put money in your account on the first day you got locked up so that you could call home. Why haven't you?"

He was sitting right in front of her, her knight in shining armor. In this quick second, she knew everything would be okay. Whenever Chink showed up, things always went right. She picked up the receiver, took a deep breath, and exhaled. "Hey, big head, I missed you, too. How are the kids? Have you found Goldie?"

Chink had been working on only two to three hours of sleep before Jordyn got locked up because he didn't want to leave her side. He was helping her look for Goldie and run her business. Even though she had Whyte and the other guys, she still needed her own muscle on hand. She was a walking prey; these slimy ass niggas would prey on her way before they went to the head of the organization just because she was a woman.

Having Dent's sorry ass around was kind of like protection because everybody always thought that he was the breadwinner and she was just wifey. But with him on the other side and Goldie missing, she was like a moving target. It was only a matter of time before people knew her role as the only woman in one of the most prominent drug rings in the state.

"The kids are fine, they are just worried about you. Between Lucky and me, they are straight. You know Destiny is like a little grown lady, so she ensures that Peace and Joi are good. I paid a lawyer, and he came to visit you last week, but you refused. How will anybody be able to help you if you refuse to take visits?"

Jordyn smiled. Her little sister always reminded her of herself. She cared for her kids well, just like Jordyn had always cared for her and Lucky when they were growing up. She knew that she needed to talk to the lawyer. Jordyn didn't even know what in the world she was charged with. Obviously, the Feds didn't have too much information because they had not confiscated her property. So, she really needed to know why in the hell she was locked up.

"I need a young female attorney; she needs to have children and preferably grew up in the ghetto. I need somebody who can actually feel my pain. I don't need a motherfucka's sympathy. I need empathy. I need somebody to fight for me like they would do for themselves."

This is the Jordyn that he knew. She looked meek and mild, but she was neither of the two. She was a bull, and that was how she had gotten as far as she did. Chink smirked and rubbed his hands together; he liked to see her fired up.

"How is everybody else doing? Have you heard anything?" The FBI had busted the warehouse and locked up her, Whyte, Puncho, and Money. Pick and Julio had just relocated to the West Coast to handle the organization's business. She didn't know if they had a warrant out for their arrest, but she knew her baby daddy didn't and wondered why. Nobody knew she was the breadwinner; everybody outside the organization thought Dent was the man. So, how in the hell did he escape federal charges and not get caught up? The more and more she thought about all this shit, the fishier it seemed.

"You are all I got. Get me that attorney down here quick. Also, get her to bring a power of attorney so I can put you and Lucky in charge of everything while I'm here. Shit, don't stop 'cause a bitch is locked up." Jordyn stood up from the hard bench and rubbed both of her ass cheeks. She put her fingers to her lips and placed them on the plexiglass.

Chink did the same. She looked so depressed when she first walked in, but she got up to leave with fire in her eyes. They had been friends for seventeen years, and he had been in love with Jordyn for seventeen years.

"Oh, and Chink? Find my nigga please," Jordyn said before the door closed in the visitation booth.

CHAPTER 24
Credit Where Credit is Due

"Can Destiny come with us on our Daddy-Daughter date today?" Mahlayah asked her daddy as they turned into the driveway of Southwest Atlanta Christian Academy.

Head removed his dark sunglasses and rubbed his eyes. He wasn't used to getting up so early in the morning. The nanny was on vacation, and these early mornings were killing him. He had just gotten in at 5:30 a.m.; here it was 7:45, and he was back out. It was only Tuesday; he didn't know how he would last for the rest of the week. He yawned, "Yeah, she can; just make sure she checks with her parents before I pick y'all up after school."

"She doesn't have any parents," Mahlayah stated very matter-of-factly.

"Well, she needs to let whoever she lives with know she will be coming with us and ensure it is okay. You tell her to give her caregiver my number if they need to talk to me," Head said as he pulled into the unloading zone.

She lives with her brother and her sister. They are grown. Her mommy's in heaven just like mine." She took off her seatbelt and reached into the backseat to grab her backpack.

He opened his console and pulled out a bankroll. He removed the rubber band, peeled a fifty-dollar bill off, and handed it to his daughter. Head then leaned over and kissed her on the cheek. Buy you and your little friend a snack during lunch. I will see you at 4:45."

"Okay, Daddy, I love you," Mahlayah said as she jumped out of the front seat. She was always excited to go to school. Her father made her live a very sheltered life. She only had friends at school or in one of her many extracurricular activities. It was only her, her father, and the nanny at home.

You couldn't have told Head fourteen years ago that he would be a father. Or that he would be a single parent taking care of his child alone. But he was, and he had to give himself a pat on the back because he was doing a damn good job. He never let what he did outside his home affect his daughter's life. He made sure that she had the best of everything and only good influences around her. He wasn't Head, the O.G., and big homie over the Bloods; he was just Dominique Stephens, a loving father.

He checked his traps instead of going home and getting back into bed. Head had people running his shit, but he wanted to make sure that he never missed a beat when it came to knowing what was going on. The situation with kidnapping Goldie had been weighing on him because he was ready to be done with the entire situation. Dent was dragging his feet. On the first night after the club's grand opening, it became evident that Dent was treated as he needed to be treated in his past affiliations.

He wasn't worthy of being a shot caller or hustler. Head knew for a fact that not everyone was meant to be a leader. Some work for it, and some are born to be it, but Dent wasn't one. He needed to be an Indian amongst the chiefs because he wasn't cut out for the boss's life. No matter how much of a good game the nigga talked, it wasn't in him or on him.

When he pulled up to the house, he saw Turtle's Audi truck parked behind the Range Rover that Dent had been driving since he got down with him. Head never had a problem directing a nigga to the food. But he did have a problem feeding a nigga over and over again. Instead of going into the house, he pulled out his cell phone and called Turtle to come outside to discuss the situation with him. He had to clarify everything before he made his next move.

Turtle came outside and got into the truck. He had shades on even though the clouds in the sky blocked the sun from shining. Head could see that his pupils enlarged behind the tint of the Cartier frames. Head could tell that he was still high from the Molly that he had taken in the Blue Flame the night before. He inhaled and exhaled loudly. He bit his tongue; he was tired of going back and forth with Turtle about doing all the drugs. This young nigga would definitely earn a bankroll, and he would definitely go toe to toe with any and everybody, but he was a Stoner. He tried every new drug that he heard somebody talking about. He was always high on something or the other.

"Big homie, you are out too early. What's on your mind?" Turtle said as he reclined the seat back, took off the dark shades, and closed his eyes.

Head laughed to himself. He had raised Turtle well; they were in tune with one another. He could tell he had to get some shit off his chest. "Man, it's this nigga Dent. I mean, he really ain't of any use to me anymore. Is he of some use to you? I know you are making him work; I left you in charge. Is he earning his keep? I don't need any cheerleaders, I need earners."

Turtle smacked his lips and exhaled. "Tsk, I was just trying to let you feel Shorty out yourself first because you are the boss and brought him on. You are one of the smartest men I know, so I trust your judgment. I follow your lead. But he has flaws, and there is too much evidence to prove it. He ain't cut out for what we do. We bang, we make bread, and Shorty doesn't do either. Dent is supposed to be the nigga on the outside looking in."

"He said he had told me everything about Whyte's organization. That young nigga Goldie is a rider, though. I told him I would let him go if he told me everything about Whyte. Goldie got more information than Dent because he is a worker, but he didn't budge. Shorty is strong, too; he is holding on. I ain't gonna lie, I thought he would have passed away by now. He lost a lot of damn blood."

"Shorty got everything in the world to live for. I talked to him the other day. Man, I ain't gonna lie, he doesn't deserve it. This nigga Dent doesn't like him cause he's a real nigga. He did this to him because he took his bitch. They never had any beef or anything. His career was taking off. He was making a lot of bread, taking care of his kids, and from what he told me, he was taking care of that nigga Dent's kids, too. Goldie told me that he planned on proposing to his girl that night and had just talked to D.J. Scream about setting up a meeting with Rozay. Goldie is a giant compared to that nigga Dent. For real, for real." Even though Turtle was fucking his baby momma, he couldn't even knock that young nigga Goldie for being a one-hundred-percent real nigga.

"But wait a minute. Ain't dis ya girl baby daddy tho' lil bro?" Head asked with his eyebrows raised.

"Yup, but I gotta give credit where credit is due. Even Raquel said that the nigga took care of Dent kids, and hers, as well."

Head frowned, his face up. "But she was with the shit at first. Both came to us at the same time, talking bout Shorty like he was a real fuck nigga. Now, come to find out, Dent is the fuck nigga, and Raquel is just a scorned woman. This ain't what we are about. We didn't have direct beef with this man. You don't kidnap and kill a nigga cause you are trying to take his boss down. You don't kidnap and kill a nigga cause you are fucking his baby momma. Goldie wasn't studying Raquel; he told you he was about to ask his bitch to marry him."

"But the good thing is Raquel doesn't even know that we are the ones who grabbed Goldie. She thinks he is dead already. Damn, dis shit is fucked up. What in the hell are we going to do?" Turtle asked.

CHAPTER 25
Home Sweet Home

Jordyn was so happy to get home to her babies that she didn't even ask who, what, when, where, or why when the correctional officer came to her door and told her to pack it up. She rolled off the hard bottom bunk, stood up, and picked up the stuff with her personal information on it. Jordyn left everything else behind. Women were coming and going constantly. Someone would need the quick meals, snacks, and personal hygiene items. She never looked back to see if she had left anything behind. She didn't care. She was on her way to where she belonged.

Those sixty-seven days felt like years. Jordyn had started to give up hope. The only thing that kept her going was talking to the kids every evening. She stopped visiting with the attorney a month after she hired her. Jordyn told her not to visit her unless she was coming to talk to her about a court date. She never came back, and Jordyn did not call her. Chink gave her updates on the case because he was constantly in contact with the lawyer, trying to get her free.

Today was her first full day back home, and she was restless. Jordyn didn't even sleep when she arrived home last night. She took a long, hot bath, slipped on one of Goldie's undershirts and a pair of his Polo boxer briefs, and quietly crept into Destiny's room. Her three lifelines were snuggled under one another. You couldn't tell where one body ended and the other began.

Jordyn stood back and just stared at them for the longest as tears threatened to fall from her eyes. Just the thought that she couldn't have been away from them a moment longer was a wish she pushed to the back of her mind. Jordyn walked around the bed and kissed each of them lightly on the forehead. She pulled back the fuzzy comforter and got into the hot pink king-size platform bed beside Peace, whose arm she had to reposition. His leg was thrown over his sister, who wrapped her arm around Destiny. Jordyn stared at the ceiling as she silently thanked the Creator. There was nowhere in the world that she would rather be.

Everybody was telling her that she needed to be calm, and she was trying her best to do that, but her soul was uneasy. So many questions were going through her mind. Hopefully, her lawyer could answer some of them later when she visited her house.

Chink and Lucky had both just left. Jordyn knew she had to do something extra special for them, considering they had held it down for her while she was gone. The doorbell rang loudly, startling her. She had not heard that sound in so long. She padded across the floor in her Gucci Flip-flops. She had lost quite a lot of weight while she was gone. Even though her commissary stayed loaded, she never had an appetite. She was worried about the kids, her brother, and her business; the worry for Goldie never ceased.

Her belt was in the first notch on her waist in her designer jeans. They used to fit her perfectly when she bought them months ago. She had on one of Destiny's shirts; she should've put on a pair of her jeans, as well.

Through the stained glass on her front door, she saw a burst of color as she peeked to try to see who it was. Hesitant to answer, she rushed into the kitchen and retrieved one of the pistols she kept around the house. Jordyn asked who it was.

"Flower delivery for a Miss Jordyn," a man with a Spanish accent replied on the other side of the door.

A smile spread across her face as she tucked the gun in the back of her waist and pulled the t-shirt over it before opening the door.

Standing before her was an older Hispanic man with his arm loaded with red roses. She looked beyond him, and another man was sitting in the passenger seat of a white delivery van, who nodded at her. Paranoia filled her as she looked back and forth between the two men. She put her right hand behind her back on the butt of her gun.

"Where would you like me to put these, Señorita? There are many, many more," he said to her before he turned and said something to the other man in Spanish. He got out, went around the back of the van, and opened the door. He filled his arms with roses and joined him at the front door. They both looked at her with their arms loaded, wondering when she would tell them what to do with them.

Jordyn removed the pistol from her waistband. She stood with it at her side and let the two men in. They both noticed the gun at the same time. Their eyes widened as they rushed into the house.

"Put them right there on the table," she said as she pointed beyond her foyer to the great room.

The two men did as they were told. With the stoic look on the young lady's face and the pistol at her side, they raced to sit down, the small glass vases filled with red roses and baby's breath. They headed out the door and back to the van, and she was about to shut the door when the second man yelled for her to stop. Jordyn opened the door back up with her pistol drawn.

"We have many, many, more bouquets for you, Señorita," the younger man said, who was the passenger. He went and filled his arms again and returned.

Jordyn decided to step outside as they went back and forth to the van six more times. She couldn't shake the paranoia that filled her. A black-on-black Jaguar convertible pulled into the circular driveway behind the delivery van. Now she wished she hadn't rushed Chink out of the house this morning. She leaned up against one of the prominent pillars and cocked her gun. One of the deliverymen came out of the door and returned to the truck. Then another one followed.

"This is our last trip, ma'am. Someone really loves you. They ordered sixty-seven dozen of our best roses," the older Hispanic man said to her as he joined the other man at the back of the van.

Her body relaxed when she noticed it was her attorney getting out of the Jag truck. She had cut and dyed her hair since her last visit to her at the federal holding facility. Today, she dressed down, and Jordyn smiled to herself. She wore her uniform, designer jeans, an expensive white T-shirt, and a blazer.

"I see somebody is happy that you are home," she said as she flashed her movie star smile at Jordyn when she noticed the two men with arms loaded with vases of roses.

CHAPTER 26
The Pop Up

Weakened by the relentless chemotherapy, Mercedes made her way to the front door of her penthouse condo. The doorbell's persistent chime echoed through the quiet space. Despite her profound fatigue, she had just roused from sleep less than thirty minutes ago. The physical toll of her treatment was evident, yet her mental fortitude remained intact, even in her husband's absence. Despite her appreciation for the solitude, Mercedes longed for the simple comforts of having Heavyn or Dejah at home to help.

She peeped through the hole, wondering why the concierge hadn't called her first to tell her she had a guest. That was one of the benefits of staying in this building and having security and a concierge, among other things. Maybe they had the wrong door.

Carmen Porter's insides were Jell-O as she pressed the doorbell. She wiped her sweaty palms down the front of her black pencil skirt, flipped her hair over her shoulder, and smiled when she heard the female voice on the other side ask who it was. This was her daughter, her adult daughter, who had a daughter of her own now. She remembered her delight when her private investigator told her she was a granddaughter. Her life had been empty for almost two years. Now, she had a family.

She asked who it was, but she opened the door once she saw a sharply dressed black woman through the peephole. She wasn't expecting anyone, so she knew she had to be lost because Mercedes had never seen her. "Yes, ma'am, can I help you?"

"I'm looking for Mercedes," she said to the young lady who came to the door. A chill swept over her as she realized that she was sick. She could tell from the gray color of her skin, the dark circles under her eyes, her sunken cheeks, and the scarf on her head. Mercedes didn't look like any of the photos the private detective had shown her. Carmen bit her bottom lip to try to contain herself. She wanted to cry; cancer had killed her mother, grandmother, and two of her aunts in her native country. It was like a ghost that haunted her. She got tested three times a year because no matter how healthy she felt, the fear resided in her that it was gonna sneak up on her like a thief in the night.

She stared at the beautiful chocolate woman with dark hair that looked like silk flowing over her shoulders. Her eyes were just as dark; they looked like black diamonds, shining just as bright as her smile. The same hair, eyes, smile, and face as hers and as her daughter's. The only difference between them was that Mercedes's skin was light. She grabbed the doorjamb and started to feel light-headed. She had imagined this moment ever since she could remember. Ever since she had Heavyn, who was her spitting image, she felt like she might look like her mother, too. As she stood on her doorstep in the flesh, she had all the confirmation she needed.

"I'm... wait, are you okay?" Carmen panicked as she saw her sway and grabbed hold of the doorjamb to steady herself.

"I know who you are," Mercedes said, her voice dripping with venom. She wobbled a little as she leaned into the doorjamb. Mercedes always imagined that meeting her mother would be different. She wanted to be happy, but all the shit that she had been through in her life prevented her from forgetting that she had been left on the steps of a church.

When she reached out to help her. Her daughter looked at her hand, which touched her arm like fire. She jerked back abruptly and almost fell. "Mercedes, I'm sorry. I didn't know that you were sick. The private detective didn't tell me. I have been looking for you for almost a year." Tears fell from her eyes.

"A whole year? Wow? Are those tears of happiness and pity, or are those that you are shedding because you did this? You gave me cancer, didn't you?" Mercedes straightened up, turned around, and entered her condo, leaving Carmen in the doorway.

She didn't know if she should follow her into her house. She stood still, staring after her as the tears fell from her eyes nonstop. Carmen remembered seeing her mother perish before her eyes, and she thought that there was nothing worse than having cancer until she heard someone say that she was the reason that they might have it.

"Don't just stand there with my door open. Come in and leave your shoes in the foyer," Mercedes said as loudly as she could as she stood at her kitchen counter, grinding fresh wheatgrass that she had gotten from her makeshift garden on her balcony before the doorbell rang. She wanted to tell her to get the hell on and return to wherever she had been the last twenty-eight years. But she had so many questions, and her being sick with cancer was one of the main reasons she asked her to stay.

For some odd reason, Mercedes had always thought that her mother was white and her father was black. That was one of the only things she thought she knew about her parents. Mercedes laughed while pouring the wheatgrass juice into two tiny teacups. She closed her eyes and prayed for healing. She immediately drank one and put the other under an ultraviolet light to boost its potency.

Carmen took off her signature blood-bottomed stilettos and walked down the hall toward where she thought Mercedes' voice was coming from. She didn't expect the condo to be as big as it was. The kitchen was almost the same size as hers was in her seven-bedroom home in Maryland. She watched as Mercedes moved slowly around the kitchen. The silence was deafening. She just wanted her to say something to her, anything. She wanted to know what she thought of her showing up at her door.

Mercedes couldn't waste her physical or mental energy being mad. This could be a blessing in disguise. She knew that what you put out, you got back, so the last thing she was trying to do was put any negative energy into the atmosphere. "Can I get you something? Coffee, tea, soda, water?"

"You have green tea?" Carmen asked.

Mercedes laughed lightly. She knew she had green tea. Green tea contains properties that can stop cancer from growing. If she knew then what she knew now about all of the things that are found in food that can prevent cancer from growing and or promote it, she would've been eating differently. But then, she didn't know that she would get breast cancer at the age of twenty-seven. She got out different canisters of various flavors of Teavana green tea, sweeteners, a teapot, and a tea set.

"Don't you just love Teavana? It is my favorite brand." Carmen could hear the nervousness in her own voice. She sat down at one of the barstools around the island. Carmen wanted to assist Mercedes because she knew that even small tasks could take a lot of energy. She didn't want to overstep her boundaries. She was happy that Mercedes had even opened the door to her and invited her into her home.

Carmen chose to come early in the day because she didn't want Mercedes' daughter to be at home. She wasn't sure what she had told her, but she knew that would have made the situation even more awkward.

"Can you help me carry this into the sitting room so that I can get more comfortable?" Mercedes asked as she picked up the tin with the rock sugar and the jar with the white gold honey and walked out of the kitchen.

Carmen followed behind her with the tea on a silver serving tray. "Your home is beautiful," she said, glancing around at the stark white furniture and plush carpet offset by black walls with silver crown molding. The private detective had told her that Mercedes and her husband were well off and that she was a much sought-after stylist to the stars all around the country.

"Thank you," she replied quietly as she sat on the chaise lounge and put her feet up. Mercedes exhaled lightly and then muttered damn out loud as she remembered that she had not taken her medication this morning.

"What's wrong? Is everything alright? You need help getting more comfortable?" Carmen rushed to Mercedes' side as soon as she set the tray on the chrome and glass cocktail table.

"I'm okay, just realized that I have not taken my medication yet." She sat up slowly and started to get up from where she was seated.

"I will get it for you. Where is it located?" Carmen said as she saw the fatigue in her daughter's eyes.

Mercedes directed her to the master bedroom and told her to get the pill bottles and a water bottle off her nightstand. Even though she was her birth mother, she was still a stranger. Mercedes knew things would not go down like this if she weren't sick. She probably wouldn't even have let her into her house. She wondered if it was a sign from God that she showed up when no one was there.

So many questions went through her mind. She didn't even know where to start. Mercedes heard her footsteps coming up the hall. She was still somewhat in shock. She couldn't believe her mother was in her house and that she looked just like her.

"You wouldn't believe me if I told you I have that same bed in my condo," Carmen said to Mercedes. She had moved from her family's home shortly after the accident because she couldn't rest well there with all of the memories.

"Really, well, we got more in common than the same face," Mercedes said sarcastically as she opened the pill bottles one after one.

"Yes, I was quite shocked when I saw your photos. All of our features are identical. I always imagined that you would look different... more like him." In her nervousness, Carmen drank the hot tea fast instead of sipping slowly.

Mercedes sat in silence; so many questions filled her head. But none of them seemed to come out as she stared at her birth mother. So many feelings filled her heart, but none of them was hatred. If anything, she longed for all the things she missed during her life because she didn't have a mother's love. Her phone rang, and she answered it as soon as 'No caller ID' flashed across the screen.

She held her head up because she felt the intense stare coming from Mercedes. "Are you comfortable? Is there anything else that I can get you? Is there anything that you want to ask me?"

"Hey baby, I caught you at a bad time? Who is that?" Money said to his wife when he didn't hear her speak, yet an unfamiliar voice was in the background.

Mercedes swallowed hard, took a deep breath, and answered her husband's question. "My mother."

CHAPTER 27
Referral Appointments

"I'm so tired. My damn feet hurt," Chrissy said as she sat down in the chair beside Pretty and took off her Gucci loafers, rubbing her feet.

"Go to the back and sit in one of those massage chairs and soak your feet. Ain't no use in complaining if you are not going to do nothing about it," Pretty said, heading to the supply closet and getting out materials for the next customer.

"Yeah, you are right. It is too damn early in the morning to be feeling like I have already done an eight-hour shift. I don't see how women get pregnant over and over and over. This is definitely my first and last one."

Pretty smiled from ear to ear. He was so happy that Chrissy had decided to continue her pregnancy. He hates that Whyte found out about it after he was locked up. The fact that they were not on good terms when he got busted didn't stop Chrissy from doing everything in her power to get her husband the best lawyers and going to visit him every visitation day.

"I'm a little early. My name is Imani; I have an appointment with Pretty for a sew-in," The petite caramel-colored girl said as she walked into the salon, slowly looking around.

"Hi, I'm Pretty. It's a pleasure to meet you. Could you just sign in over there on the log? My assistant will be here in a few minutes to wash your hair. Can I get you anything to drink? Soda, fruit juice, wine?" Pretty said as he put supplies on his workstation.

"No, I'm fine, thank you for asking. It is beautiful in here. I didn't realize it was this big. You sure can't tell from the outside. I ride by this place all the time," Imani said as she sat on the sofa before the salon.

"Were you referred by one of my regular customers? Because I do give referral discounts." Pretty looked the girl over; she was dressed simply, but her Chanel bag, loafers, and jewels screamed money.

"One of the girls I follow on Instagram posted a picture, and her sew-in looked so natural. She tagged you, and I booked the first available appointment. I can't even remember who it was. I'm sure it will come to me soon."

He finally listened to Chrissy and hired an assistant. She was a big help because she shampooed and conditioned the hair and braided up all his sew-ins for him. That gave Pretty more time to do more heads. Now everything was running like a top. His assistant, Pinky, walked in with her hands full. She had a cup carrier and a paper bag from Starbucks. Pretty smiled and rushed over to help her with some of her stuff.

"Good morning, Good morning, Good morning. I got everybody's favorite. Where is Ms. Chrissy? I got her something extra special today," Pinky said as she headed toward the back with a Venti Matcha with almond milk and no whipped cream. Chrissy had just discovered that dairy products were making her sick.

"She is in the spa area; I think she is in one of those massage chairs. Poor child is tired already, and she ain't done a lick of work. Thank God she is the boss lady," Pretty said.

Imani's eyes followed Pinky as she walked toward the back. "Oh, so this is really a spa? I just thought that was the name of the salon. How quaint, I think I might get a massage or facial or something before I leave."

"Yes, ma'am, we are a full-blown spa. Our massage therapist will be in after twelve p.m., and our esthetician is already on duty," Pretty said to his new client.

The door opened, and a familiar face walked in. Pretty stared because he couldn't place where he knew her from. "How can I help you?"

"Yes, I would like a keratin treatment and a cut. I've been dying for you to put your hands in my head," the young lady said, smiling brightly at Pretty.

"You look so familiar. I just can't put my hand on where I know you from. Please forgive me. What is your name?" Pretty asked the young lady.

"I'm Chaney Smith. My husband is best friends with the owner's husband. I met you at the grand opening of Luxurious. I'm, I'm, I'm Dude's wife," she stuttered nervously. Although she hated her husband, he was still her husband. Chaney knew no other way to identify herself without saying Dude's name.

"Hey, beautiful, I knew I remembered you from somewhere. I know I was drunk that night, but I remember you and your badass dress. I heard that you were in a bad car accident. How are you doing? Have a seat," Pretty said to Chaney; something told him to look at the girl, Imani. She had a stank look on her face when she sat down beside her.

"I'm ready for you, you can follow me this way," Pinky said to Imani when she returned to the front.

Imani stood up, removing her blue jean jacket, and her round belly protruded from under her extra-small top. She rubbed her stomach and smiled before she hung her coat on the rack.

"Oh, my! Look at you, aren't you the cutest? How far along are you?" Pretty said when he noticed that his customer was expecting.

"I just turned eight months. I didn't realize how small this damn shirt was when I put it on. It might have shrunk on the ride over," Imani said, heading into the spa area when the assistant came and directed her to the shampoo room. She just wanted to get a glance at Chrissy.

Months had passed since she spoke to Whyte, and now that he was locked up, she had no contact with him. He had yet to reach out to her, even though she had written him letter after letter. Her coming to the salon was the last straw. She knew that once she came clean to his wife, Chrissy would go back and tell Whyte, and then he would call her.

As she sat down in the shampoo chair and got the best shampooing she ever had, she thought about what she would say to Chrissy. The fact that Whyte had stayed away from her because he was trying to save his marriage made Imani hate his wife, even though she had never done anything wrong to her. She had told him that she didn't have a problem with him living a double life. But no, he had to go and throw her and her baby away. He acted like they didn't exist anymore. Well, now she would prove to him that they had done it.

Pretty decided to go ahead and wash Chaney's hair so he could get both of his customers out before the next one came in. They went into the shampoo room, and he washed her hair, put the keratin treatment on it, and set her under the dryer. Then he went back to check on Chrissy. She had dozed off in the massage chair. He dipped his finger in the water, and it got cold. He shook her gently.

"Girl, get your butt up. Do you have anyone on your schedule? You should just go home."

"I have two chemical peels later on, and my intern is coming in today. Bitch, I'm tired as hell, though. This baby is taking all of my energy. I thought it was supposed to get better as I get further along," Chrissy said as she stretched and bent down to dry her wet feet off.

"It is getting better; your ass ain't throwing up everywhere. You are going to complain this whole pregnancy, aren't you?" Pretty said as he helped Chrissy out of the chair. He could see her little baby bump sticking out, but she acted like she was nine months old. He hoped he survived because it was apparent that his best friend would drive him up the wall.

"You're right; I would rather be sleepy all the time than throw up everywhere. Where is my green tea? I know that will give me a little boost of energy." Chrissy slipped her feet into her shoes and headed toward the front.

"Oh, and I got a walk-in customer I know you want to see." Pretty pointed toward the other side of the shampoo room at someone under the dryer.

"Who in the world is that?" Chrissy asked as she looked at the person, rigid; she couldn't tell because half of their face was blocked from her view.

"That is Dude's wife, chile," Pretty said in a loud whisper.

"For real? Whyte and I were just talking bout her. Thank God she is alright. That nigga did her so damn wrong. I meant to tell you about it, but fell asleep after he told me."

"Oh, my fucking gosh! You know you are supposed to give me the tea. Now your ass is a narcoleptic and shit, and I'm missing out. Tell me what happened," Pretty said as he pulled Chrissy back in the back.

"You can spend the night with Mercedes and me, and we will talk then. Go handle your customers before you have a shop full of damn folks." She pulled away from Pretty and headed to greet the customers and offer them refreshments.

Imani gritted her teeth and shut her eyes as she tried to deal with the pain from getting the cornrows from Pinky. She was tender-headed, and this reminded her of getting her hair braided when she was a kid. She opened her eyes when she heard a familiar voice. It was Chrissy; she knew it even though the voice didn't match her appearance. Her eyes bulged out of her head.

"She doesn't look like what I thought she would."

Always on the defense, Pretty's neck snapped fast as he looked over at his client in the salon chair next to where he was standing. "What did you say? Who doesn't look like what you thought?" He looked around, trying to see who she was talking about because he knew she wasn't talking about Chrissy. He didn't see anybody; he followed the direction of her view, and it was Chrissy.

"You know her?" Pinky asked Imani as she turned the salon chair around to get a better angle to finish the braiding.

She started stuttering, and she felt Pretty's glare on her, but what made her lose her words was Chrissy's baby bump. No wonder he didn't want her baby; it was because his wife was pregnant, too.

"We got something in common," Imani blurted out in anger.

"Honey, what y'all got in common 'cause I don't know you," Pretty shouted, attracting Chrissy's attention from across the room.

"What you got going on over here, chile? You still cussing me out for falling asleep on you?" Chrissy said joining Pretty.

"This young lady seems to think you two have something in common. Do you know her 'cause I sure as hell don't?" Pretty asked, snapping his neck back and forth, looking between Imani and Chrissy.

Chrissy looked at her hard; she'd never seen her before. But looking down at her stomach, she instantly knew who she was. "Bitch, and I do mean bitch, you got some motherfucking nerve bringing your trifling ass in my place of business. I have been warning you for months. I said I don't play about my money, and I don't play about my man, and from the looks of it, you fucking with both of them. I'm going to count to five, and you better be on the other side of the door. At the count of ten, your vehicle needs to be off my property before I beat that baby out of your motherfucking ass."

"Bitch! Who do you think you are? You ain't no better 'cause he chose you first. If he hadn't met your big black ass, we would be together. The only reason he is with you is because of loyalty. You were there from the start. Whyte is in love with me. This is his child right here, and it was made from love," Imani said as she stood up from the salon chair.

Chrissy swung her right fist, instantly knocking Imani to the floor. She started kicking her repeatedly.

Pretty was shocked and frozen in place. He couldn't believe what was happening.

The timer stopped on the dryer, and Chaney lifted the hood. She heard the commotion. Pretty was standing in place with his mouth agape, watching Chrissy repeatedly kick someone on the floor, balled up in the fetal position. Chaney yanked her arm hard and ducked when Chrissy swung at her.

"It's me, Chaney. Stop it, stop it right now! Please," she pleaded with Chrissy as she pulled her to the back of the salon.

CHAPTER 22
Rice Street

Mercedes paced back and forth in the lobby of Fulton County Jail. She had signed the bond earlier. She didn't know what was taking so long for them to release Chrissy. She looked down at her phone and saw that it was her husband. She pressed ignore. She would talk to Money after she had some good news.

Tameka sat there and wrung her hands. She rushed over to the jail when she found out that Chrissy had been locked up for assault and battery. Tameka was so out of the loop. She didn't even know that Chrissy was pregnant. Tameka had been living in her own bubble. With the bust getting so much attention on the news and social media, and everybody knowing that was her husband, she became introverted. She got tired of people asking her questions about everything.

"Girl, sit down and save some of your energy. She has never been in trouble; they don't have any type of hold on her. Chrissy will be down in a little while," Pretty said to Mercedes.

"Who is this bitch? Where in the hell did she come from?" Tameka asked out loud to no one in particular.

"She came out of the woodwork, obviously, as they all do when they get tired of playing the background. The little bitch had too much nerve, though. She should have learned more about Chrissy beyond her workplace. Because if she'd done a background check, she would've known that she wasn't one to be fucked up with. It's one thing to play on the phone, but to come into a bitch business taking all that bullshit. That bitch got what she deserved," Mercedes replied.

"I couldn't believe what I was seeing. Chrissy was just kicking her and kicking her over and over. Everybody else seemed to be frozen in place," Chaney said.

"Hell, I was frozen in place! If you hadn't come in there when you did, Chrissy's ass might be locked up for murder cause she was kicking that bitch ass literally for old and new. That is why I say you just can't fuck with people, because you don't know what the hell they have going on underneath the surface. I honestly believe she could have kicked that girl to death," Pretty said, feeling bad because he didn't stop Chrissy; he could've stopped her before she even hit the girl.

"Well, thank God you were there," Tameka said to Chaney.

"We all need a damn vacation. It's a wonder she is the only one that has spazzed out and beat a bitch. Lord knows I'm fed up. The only reason I haven't is that I'm too damn tired. This chemotherapy is whipping my ass. I went from having one or two bad days a week to having one or two good days per week," Mercedes said when she finally sat down in one of the hard chairs.

A girl walked in and went up to the desk. She had on a hoodie and a pair of shades. All the girls' eyes followed her because her body was bananas, even though they couldn't see how she looked. Pretty let out a whistle low and long.

"I know real, and I bet you all that is real. She is collard greens and cornbread fed. I bet she is from Perry Homes or some shit."

Mercedes burst out laughing. "You're so damn silly. Why does she gotta be from my hood, though? But I can tell that her ass is real. It giggles in her leggings when she walks. She is bad; look at her waist. She made up like you, Chaney."

"Yeah, Chaney bitch you're fine. If I were fine like you, I would've been a stripper even if I had money. I would just want everybody to see me naked. Girl, I saw you at that party. Your titties sit up like a fifteen-year-old virgin, and that ass, I swear it, was sculpted. If I weren't so damn pretty myself, I probably would've paid you to be my beard, too. At least your husband has good taste." Pretty was about to continue, but Mercedes slapped him hard on his arm.

"You fix your mouth to say any damn thing. You just don't know when to shut up," Mercedes said to Pretty as she looked at Chaney. She saw the sadness in her eyes.

Chaney's eyes welled up with tears, but she fought them back. She knew that Pretty didn't mean any harm. The truth hurt like hell, and nobody knew the whole truth except her and her mother. The young lady sat down and removed the hoodie. Even though several years had passed, she still looked the same. It was her old friend Debbie.

"Debbie-Cakes, is that you?"

She took the shades off her face and turned around, and she just reached and grabbed her long-lost friend in a tight embrace. "Oh, my God, Chaney, I have missed you so damn much, girl," Debbie-Cakes said through tears.

"I told you she was fine like a stripper," Pretty murmured under his breath to Tameka and Mercedes.

Mercedes hit him even harder this time, but she couldn't help but giggle.

Chaney broke the embrace; she wiped the tears from her face and then from Debbie's. "What are you doing down here?"

"My son got locked up for fighting his daughter's mama's boyfriend for jumping on her. It's a whole bunch of mess. Why are you down here? Dude?"

"He's down here, but I'm not down here for him. One of my girl-friends just made bail, so we are all waiting for her to get released. This is my girl Tameka, my girl Mercedes, and my girl Pretty. You guys, this is one of my oldest and dearest friends, Debbie," Chaney said, smiling with one arm still wrapped tightly around Debbie's shoulder.

Chrissy limped over to them unnoticed. She was so happy that she wouldn't have to wait for someone to pick her up. She cleared her throat to get their attention.

Everyone jumped up at once and rushed up to her. All of them started talking at once. "Are you alright?"

"I'm okay. I'm just hungry, and I think I broke my toe," Chrissy said as she pushed her hair off her face and limped toward the door.

"Let's get her checked out quickly, fed, and home to her bed so she can get some rest," Pretty said to everyone.

"I ain't got no home. Home is where the heart is, and I don't have a heart anymore," Chrissy said, holding her head down as she walked out the front door of 901 Rice Street.

No one said anything, and it seemed no one knew what to say as they walked out following Chrissy.

Chaney stayed behind for a few minutes as everyone piled into her G-wagon. "I just want to apologize for everything that I said. Even after realizing it was true, I was too stubborn to humble myself, apologize, and admit that you were right. I want you to know that your words saved my life, and I will forever love you, and you will always be one of my dearest friends. I need to go and see about my girl, but here is my number. Promise me that you will call me tomorrow. We can meet up after Pretty finally finishes my hair."

Debbie-Cakes just shook her head yes. She was at a loss for words. Everything happened for a reason; she probably wouldn't have seen Chaney if her son hadn't gotten locked up. She pulled out her cell phone and handed it to her so she could put her number in it. Then she got up and gave her a hug before she walked out.

She looked back one last time, waved, and blew her a kiss before signaling for her to call her.

CHAPTER 20
All In Vain

Head was mad at himself. He obviously didn't think things out, and now he was going behind himself, fixing what he had fucked up. He was going to leave things as they were, but after talking to Goldie that day and Destiny joining him and his daughter on their outing, he knew he didn't have a choice. He pulled the strings and got Jordyn released; now he had to get rid of Dent and free Goldie.

Three days earlier, he had a private doctor who he kept on his payroll come over and check Goldie out. The doctor was shocked at how Goldie's body had basically healed itself. While everyone was gone, he administered an antibiotic injection and vitamins, along with hydration via I.V. Head had Turtle and Dent working in the field more lately, and they had been sticking close to the spot. He had gained so much respect for Goldie and his whole movement. He was even looking at Whyte in a different light. Head had fucked up bad, and it weighed on him heavily.

He got up, went to the front door, and opened it. Head had called Dee to see what could be done to clean this mess up. He needed two heads because he wasn't thinking right with one. "Man, why the fuck do you never stop me when I'm coming up with this shit?"

"Everything always works out. Plus, you have never fucked up this bad," Dee said as he came in and sat down across from his friend.

"So, did you think it was a fucked idea when I came to you with it?" he asked as he took his red fitted hat off and threw it on the floor. Head was sweating profusely. He took his red bandana from his back pocket and wiped the sweat off his face and bald head.

"Nope, not initially, but when I found out that Ol' boy didn't tell the truth about shooting the youngin', it didn't feel right anymore. It made me question everything he had told you. You feel what I'm saying?" Dee responded.

"Yup, that is exactly how I was feeling. I felt like everything Dent might have said was a lie. Then, when I started spending time with the youngin', I found out my feelings were factual. Everything Ol' Boy had said was a lie. He was just trying to make himself look good." He got up, glanced out the window, and stared into the darkness. He had gotten Jordyn out of jail and sent her a dozen roses for every day that she was locked up. But he knew that wouldn't make up for the days away from her kids or the money that she missed. She was a hell of a woman, and he saw why both of them niggas were crazy about her. She was the best in every world. If only he had met her under different circumstances.

"So, what is the plan? I know one thing for sure: I gotta get rid of that nigga Biggs. He is getting on my nerves. I can't put him back in prison cause he is going to run his mouth. I'mma have to off him."

"It's a wonder they haven't had him killed yet. Everybody in the warehouse got busted, but he got out the next day. They got to know that he set them up."

"Oh, they know he is hiding, and ain't nobody on the streets but the girl," Dee said, speaking of Jordyn.

"From what I heard of her, she will do him with no hesitation. They say she ain't afraid to shoot," Head said, laughing; the more he thought about her, the more he had to talk himself out of pursuing her for himself.

"Well damn, I guess you should be happy that she hasn't come for you yet, the big homie." Dee got up and went into the kitchen to get a bottle of water from the refrigerator. His phone rang; he cleared his throat and answered it in his professional tone.

"Special Agent DeAunte Johnson," he answered, then listened to the other end. He hung up the phone and shook his head.

"What, what is wrong now, Special Agent Johnson?" Head said, sarcastically.

"All this shit has been in vain, all of it!" he replied to Head as he plopped down on the sofa with his head in his hands.

"Don't hold out on me. What is going on? It's something with them niggas?" Curiosity was killing Head.

Dee jumped off the sofa. "Let the Youngin' go; I gotta figure out how to get the rest of the folks out. They weren't stopping you from getting money. They were your supplier. El Pappito had put Whyte over all the work coming in from the West Coast. The call I just got said that over four hundred million dollars in sales have ceased since they have been locked up."

Head banged his fist on the coffee table so hard that one of the legs flew off. "Man, what the fuck? How come we didn't know that? I thought he was getting his work from another Mexican name, Ponchees."

"Ponchees is what they call him on the East Coast; they are one and the same. We gotta fix this shit, A.S.A.P., before they find us in little pieces cut up," Dee said as he was leaving out the door.

"Okay, you go do what you gotta do. I'mma free the youngin' and off Dent. Call me if you need me," Head said as he put all the locks on the door.

* * *

Goldie heard the locks twisting; he took the earplugs out of his ears and pushed the pad and iPod under the pillow as he sat on the bed. When he saw it was Head, he pulled it back out. "I was working on a hit, and the beat came to me in my sleep. I jumped up and started writing. I hope I don't forget the beat before I get back in the studio."

"Is that usually how it always happens? You hear a beat in your head, and then you start to write?" Head asked as he sat down on the stool beside the bed.

"Actually, this is the first time that it happened. I don't do beats. Either Lucky comes with the beats, or people send them to me. I just write the lyrics. Now those come to me in my sleep, or I could be going through something, and I will just start writing."

Seems pretty dope. I got some good news, and I got some bad news. Which one do you want first?" Head said to the young guy, whom he had grown very fond of.

"Give me the bad news first." Goldie knew that Head had started being nice to him, but business was still business. He knew that he had been brought to this house to die.

"I'm not going to be seeing you much anymore," Head said solemnly.

"Can you do me a favor? Please ensure my girl gets the notebook and the ring in the pocket of the jeans I had on when I came. It's a goodbye letter and instructions on how I want everything to be handled. And can you just wait until I go to sleep and shoot me point-blank range? I don't wanna suffer." Goldie couldn't stop the few tears that fell from his eyes.

Head bit his lip. Shorty was just as thorough as it came. "Ain't no need for all that, my nigga. I'm bout to let you go home to your old lady and your kids. I just need you to do me one solid, my nigga, cause this shit is way bigger than me and Whyte, my dude. I need you to tell every-body that it was Dent by himself, just leave me and my crew out of it. I promise I'm working on getting your other folks out like I did your old lady, and I'mma make sure Dent is the least of your worries. Can you handle that?"

"You got my word, Blood. You looked out for me. You could've let me die, but you didn't. You made sure my ol' lady got home to those kids safe. I don't owe you one, but I'mma make sure you straight. And don't worry bout Dent. I wanna handle that nigga by myself, face-to-face," Goldie said; he couldn't hide the excitement from his voice.

"Well, come on, let me take you home," Head said as he got out of the chair, ready to head out of the room.

"Damn, I don't even have any shoes. Don't worry about it, I'll go barefoot. Just get me to my baby," Goldie said gleefully as he walked out of the room with the bloody clothes that he had thrown over his arm and the notebook that he had been writing in his hand.

CHAPTER 30
Westside Girls

C hrissy limped into the townhouse and immediately put the security code in. It still smelled like fresh paint. She hadn't been on this property since she did the move-out inspection.

"This is really nice. Are all of your properties this nice?" Mercedes asked as she followed Chrissy and Pretty into the townhouse. She looked around, and it looked even larger on the inside.

"So, what are you going to do about furniture? Will you bring some stuff from the other house or go furniture shopping?" Pretty asked. He was strictly against Chrissy moving out of the mansion, but she wasn't trying to hear what he said.

"If you are going furniture shopping, then I'm your girl. We can go into the apparel mart and get some shit that the stores don't even have," Mercedes said excitedly.

"Actually, all I need is a bed, a nightstand, and a desk for my computer, and I'm good," Chrissy said as she walked around the house and opened some windows to let the paint smell out.

"If you say so, honey. You are mad at your husband, and you are punishing yourself. You think I would've left my big ass house cause the nigga cheated on me. He ain't even in the house, Chrissy. What point are you proving by leaving your home, and he ain't there? He locked up. You could be sleeping in your big, comfortable California king double pillow top and tell him that you moved out, and he wouldn't know the difference.

"Why you gotta be so damn extra all the time, Pretty? It's the principle of things. The house is filled with memories that she is obviously trying to get away from. Have a heart, Damnit," Mercedes said, punching Pretty in the shoulder.

"I got some furniture in the storage area in the basement. I might have some stuff down there that I can use. It has been so long I can't remember."

Chrissy said as she walked toward the door leading downstairs to the basement.

"Yeah, you must check before entering the store and repurchasing the same stuff. How long has this place been empty?" Mercedes said as she followed behind Chrissy down the narrow steps.

"About three or four months, I think. Girl, I forget which ones are occupied and which are not since I hired a property manager. I used to handle everything myself. But when the spa's business started booming, I hired someone so that I could dedicate more time to the spa."

"Girl, this has a full basement. Why didn't you let me get this one? Bitch, you are so petty. I could be down here doing hair and shit," Pretty said when he hit the bottom stair. He stood there and looked around in amazement.

"You got a shop to do hair in, silly ass lil' girl." Chrissy turned on the lights and looked around. It looked like her tenants didn't even use the basement. The bucket of paint, ladder, and floor wax were still where she had left them. She removed them from the front of the door and opened it. She realized the light bulb had blown when she flicked the light switch.

"Wait a minute, here you go." Mercedes went into her pocketbook and handed Chrissy a small flashlight.

Chrissy twisted the top of the small flashlight and was shocked at the power of it. It lit up the whole room. What was even more shocking was that the room was empty, with no furniture in it. In its place were wooden crates everywhere.

"Oh, you haven't opened the stuff yet? You should be able to furnish the place with all this, or at least a few rooms. Heavyn and I love putting furniture together. You just got to catch me when I have some energy," Mercedes said as she looked at all the wooden crates.

"Shhhhhhhh," Chrissy said as she backed out of the storage room and started to close the door.

"Bitch, don't be shushing nobody. Why are you looking like you just saw a ghost?" Pretty whispered softly, not wanting to disturb the storage area, as he was too busy taking in the large basement.

"What is wrong, Chris? Why are you looking like that?" Mercedes said to her friend, whose eyes had doubled in size.

"Girl, that is not furniture. That is dope. All those damn crates are filled with cocaine," Chrissy said as she rushed toward the steps. She was trying to hurry up and get out of the house. She was scared and didn't know what was happening, but she wanted to get far away from the townhouse.

Pretty and Mercedes were on her tail, heading up the steps just as fast. When they got to the top of the steps, Chrissy slammed the basement door extra hard. She opened the front door to let her friends out in silence. She then turned on the alarm, pulled the door up, and locked it.

When Chrissy hopped behind the wheel of her truck, her friends were staring at her. She exhaled deeply. "Lord, have mercy, Jesus! Why didn't he tell me? What am I going to do with all that? What if, What if, What if?" she stammered. She put her head on the steering wheel and sighed loudly.

"I know who we need to call. You can take the girl out of the west side, but you can't take the west side out of the girl," Mercedes said from the passenger's seat.

Chrissy and Pretty said it at the same time, "Jordyn!"

"You damn right," Mercedes said, smiling as they rode down the street. She leaned forward and turned the radio on.

The sounds of Future's 'Move dat dope' flooded the truck. They all laughed, threw their hands up in the air, and bobbed their heads back and forth.

CHAPTER 31
Never Broke Again

Jordyn had cooked a big dinner every night since she came home from jail. Being away from her family made her realize that she needed to focus more of her energy on them than on money because she had legitimate businesses that made money. Jordyn wasn't hurting for cash. But she was just afraid of ever being broke again. Tonight, she took requests from the kids; they all agreed they wanted spaghetti and meatballs.

She put the garlic bread in the oven, went to the sink, and washed her hands. She was worried about Chink; she hadn't seen him since this morning. Jordyn picked up the phone and called her little brother. He answered on the first ring; she heard the music in the background. He was in the studio. Since everyone found out that he was the one who made Goldie's beats, Lucky has always worked. His buzz had passed the city now. He was on his way to the top.

"Hey, sis, I'm bout finished here. I will be over for dinner in about thirty minutes," Lucky told his sister. He made it his business to stop whatever he was doing every day to go and eat dinner with his family.

"Okay, Lucky, but I was calling you about Chink. I haven't talked to him since this morning. Have you talked to him this evening? When I called, his phone went straight to voicemail." Jordyn was trying her best not to worry.

"He is straight; he is just handling some things. Don't worry bout him. You might look up, and he will be sitting at the table eating dinner, too," Lucky said; he heard the fear in his sister's voice.

Jordyn ended the call with her little brother, put her phone in her back pocket, and headed up the stairs to tell the kids to wash up for dinner. As usual, they were all in the same room. She loved how close the three of them were. Peace and Joi were both jumping on the bed, and Destiny was sitting on the beanbag watching a movie on the Disney Channel.

"Mommy, I know a secret. But you can't tell nobody," Peace said as he bounced off the bed, came up, and wrapped his arms around his mother's waist.

"You are my main man. We do not have any secrets, buddy," Jordyn said as she kissed him on the top of his head.

"I know that is why I'm right here, about to tell you. I know who sent you all those pretty flowers downstairs," Peace said, jumping up and down.

"Who?" Jordyn was still wondering because everything the card said was "welcome home." She had assumed it was Chink, but when he saw them, he was just as surprised. She then thought that maybe Dent had done it. Jordyn left it at that. He had yet to show his face around here.

"It was Mahlayah's daddy. I heard her and Auntie Des talking about it on the iPad."

"What? Is he telling the truth, Des?" she turned around and said to her sister. She didn't say anything, and Jordyn realized that she had earbuds in her ears. Destiny was listening to music and watching television at the same time. She reached down and pulled the earbuds out of her ears.

"What? What did I do?" Destiny said, startled.

"Was it your friend's dad who sent me the roses when I got home?" Jordyn asked her sister with her hand on her hip. She looked directly into her eyes so that she would know that she meant business.

"Yes, ma'am," she answered.

"Why didn't you tell me that when you saw me racking my brain trying to figure out where they came from?" Jordyn asked her little sister.

"Because I didn't want to get in trouble for giving him our address. He is really, really nice. He is the one who bought me those K.D.s with the outfit to match. He took us out to eat and to get manicures and pedicures after school. We went shopping. Mahlayah has the best daddy. I was sad about you when I was with them, and he said that he wished he could get you out. So when you got free, I told Mahlayah, and she said she would tell her daddy. That is when she said he wanted the address so that he could send you some flowers to welcome you home." Destiny had fear in her eyes; she knew her big sister did not want anyone to know where they lived.

Jordyn wanted to explode, but she didn't. She just walked out of the room. Her little sister didn't mean any harm. Jordyn would just have to be prepared because Head knew where she lived. She had been focused on finding that nigga Biggs; she had to do something to him. He was the reason that they all got locked up to begin with.

She didn't feel right about him in the first place. But when Chink came home and told her that the barber had sent her a message telling her that Biggs got out two days after the bust, she'd been searching under every rock, high and low, for his ass. She prayed that she would find Goldie in the process. Jordyn knew in her heart that he wasn't dead. Her love was so strong for him; if he were dead, she would feel it.

As she headed down the steps to make the Caesar salad to go with dinner, there was banging at the door. She pulled her phone out of her back pocket and checked the camera at the front door. It was three people, but she couldn't tell who they were. She got her pistol out of the drawer in the foyer and went to the front door. Jordyn shook her head, thinking she needed to fence in her property and gate it off. The doorbell started to ring.

"Who is it?" Jordyn said as she tried to make out the figures through the stained glass.

"Us," the three of them said in unison.

"Us who?" Jordyn asked.

"Mercedes, Chrissy, and Pretty," Mercedes said as she looked up into the camera at the door.

Jordyn snatched the door open quickly. "Hey, y'all. What the hell bring ya' out here to my neck of the woods?"

"Can we come in?" Chrissy asked quietly.

"I'm sorry for being rude." Jordyn opened the door and let them in. She noticed Chrissy's baby bump right away. She rushed up to her and put her hand on her stomach.

Chrissy burst into tears.

"Oh lawd, you have started this bitch to crying. Do you have some Hennessey or some Dusse? It's about to be a long ass night," Pretty said as he walked past them. He started to look around.

"This bitch house is sharp as hell. No wonder they locked her ass up," he said to Mercedes like Jordyn wasn't standing right there.

Jordyn looked at Pretty and rolled her eyes. She embraced Chrissy. "I didn't mean to make you cry. I'm just surprised. My brother didn't say anything about you being pregnant. I'm about to be an auntie."

"He didn't know about this baby when he got locked up. He just knew about the other one," Chrissy said as she wiped her face.

Jordyn looked at them in shock. "Huh"

"It's a long story. We will tell you about it. But we got some business to talk about first," Pretty said.

"You mean I got some business to talk to her about. Go sit your ass down somewhere, girl. You're wrecking my nerves," Chrissy said to Pretty.

"I know you got a bar in this palace. Point me in that direction and I'm out y'all bitches way." He went in the direction she was pointing, which was down the hall.

"Bless your heart. How do you put up with her, I meant him all day long?" Jordyn asked as she led the girls into the kitchen. She washed her hands and pulled everything out of the fridge to make the salad as the girls sat on the island.

"He is all I have, and I love him. I know he will never take from me, never leave me, and never lie to me," Chrissy said to Jordyn as she got comfortable on the stool.

"Understood, that is how I feel about Chink. But he ain't gay," Jordyn said.

"If he ain't gay, then he is in love with you," Mercedes said.

"Girl, nooooooo! He has been like my best friend since I was in middle school. He doesn't look at me like that," Jordyn said, correcting her.

"Honey, you are in denial. I bet every dollar I got in the bank that he is in love with you," Mercedes said as she folded her arms across her chest.

Chrissy interrupted the conversation. "Okay, I got a room full of dope. What can you do with it?"

Jordyn's eyes bulged out of her head. "You got a room full of what?" It was a drought of cocaine and heroin. All she had been getting in was weed because she had another plug for that. This had to be the dope that Whyte was saying that he had stockpiled. She had been wondering where it was.

CHAPTER 32
What I'm After, Money Can't Buy

Chink had been sitting outside the hotel room for at least two hours, waiting for him to come out and go to the snack machine. He was on a schedule because every night at the same time, he came out, went to the vending machines, and returned with food. Tonight, he seemed to be off schedule. He looked at his watch; it was a quarter to ten, and still no sign of him. He knew he was in the room because he could see him when he got up to move around.

The door opened slightly, and he stuck his head out and looked around. When he saw the clear coast, he pulled the latch outside the door and closed it. He headed toward the vending machines. The lady at the front desk had told him that they were refilling the machines today. He hoped that they were getting something new. Being cooped up in the hotel, eating the vending food, reminded him of his commissary in jail.

Biggs was so paranoid that he was scared to order takeout. He had seen too many movies where the deliverymen turned out to be contract killers. Dee had stopped answering his phone calls. He was growing impatient with him. The last time Biggs talked to Dee, he asked about the witness protection program. He promised him that he was going to work on it.

Biggs' eyes lit up like Christmas when he saw the machine fully stocked. He started feeding it dollar after dollar and making selections. He hadn't eaten anything but a honey bun and a cup of noodles all day. Biggs loaded his arms with ten dollars' worth of snacks and prepared food and returned to his hotel room. He would drink water from the sink because he had no more singles for the soda machine.

He backed into the room, checking his surroundings before he went inside. Biggs was happy he chose the room in the back. Nobody was going or coming back here. He dumped the food on the bed and pulled the hoodie over his head. That was the last thing he remembered before he woke up naked with the sheet around his neck.

Chink sat on the bed, eating the Flaming Hot Cheetos. He had been waiting about forty-five minutes for him to wake. He had some questions that he needed the answers to before the end. "I bet you wished you just would've stayed your bitch ass in jail, don't you?

"I can pay you. All I have to do is make a phone call, and I can have you whatever you want," Biggs said, his voice shaking.

"What I'm after, money can't buy my nigga," Chink said as he stood up.

Biggs didn't realize how big he was when he was sitting down on the bed. "Whatever you want, my people can get it for you. Just let me down from here."

"Jordyn ain't gonna be at peace until you are just a memory. I'm here to make sure she doesn't get your blood on her hands," Chink said as he put his foot on the chair that Biggs was standing on.

"You are about to kill me for a bitch? Come on, dog. Take the cash and just go bout your business. I will be in the witness protection program in a few days. You can tell her you handled the situation because I will be far from Atlanta." Biggs was begging for his life. The sheet was tied tightly around his neck, and it was uncomfortable. The end had been thrown over one of the beams in the ceiling.

"She ain't the one that is a bitch. She is more solid than you ever will be." Chink yanked on the sheet a little bit.

"She wasn't even supposed to be there; it was just supposed to be

Money, Whyte, and the cop. Jordyn was in the wrong place at the wrong time. She wasn't even under the FBI's radar." Biggs tried to reach up and adjust the tightness of the sheet. He was losing circulation.

"Who do you work for? How did you get out of prison?" Chink questioned him as he tugged a little harder on the sheet.

"DeAunte came to see me in jail and said he was watching Money and Whyte them. He found Money's name as the only person sending me large sums of cash. He told me that if I could set Money up, he could get me released and get me a large sum of cash and dope." Biggs was gasping for air and becoming lightheaded.

"Who is this Dee that you keep on talking bout? He from Atlanta?" Chink asked him.

"He is an FBI agent. I think he is from Atlanta; if not, he has been here for a long time. Can you please let me down? I'm telling you everything that you want to know," Biggs pleaded to Chink.

"Yeah, I appreciate the information." Chink kicked the chair from under Biggs and picked up the chips off the bed before walking out the door.

Chink took the gloves off and threw them in the sewer before getting into his car. He picked up his phone from his console and powered it on. Nobody knew what he planned on doing today, but Lucky, so he had to call him first. He dialed his number and checked his pocket to make sure the ring was there.

"I did it. Yeah, I'm headed that way now. Oh, you're over there now. She got company? Who? Oh, okay. Yes, I'm going to ask her tonight. I think what my grandmother said yesterday was right. Jordyn will not be able to enjoy her present and future if she keeps holding onto the past." Chink was happy that his grandmother gave him her blessing when he went and talked to her about Jordyn and the children. She always did love her.

"Aight lil' bro I'mma holler at you later." Chink ended the call with a big smile on his face. He headed toward Etheridge; he had one more thing to do before he headed in for the night. It was a ghost town when he pulled up on the backside of the D' building. Raquel's car was parked in its usual spot in front of the dumpster.

Chink put his hood on his head and ran a few feet to where her car was. He didn't want his car to be placed this close to her door. He bent down and slid the small explosive under her car and ran back to his car. Chink didn't want anyone to get hurt, but he wanted the vehicle destroyed. He picked up his untraceable burnout phone and dialed 911. He told the operator that a car had just exploded in the back of the D building in Etheridge Court. He waited until he got to the top of the hill and pressed the button. When Chink heard the small explosion, a smile crept across his face.

* * *

"Alright, my dog, curbside service," Head said as he pulled up to Jordyn's house.

Goldie raised his eyebrow but didn't say anything about the fact that he came right to their front door without asking for any directions. "I sure appreciate it, man. I'm gonna get with you by the weekend. I need a few days just loving on my family."

"You should've at least let me get you some fresh clothes and shoes. This is going to be the first time you've seen them in months," Head said to Goldie. He couldn't help but feel guilty, and it was showing.

"I'm good, man. I don't care if I showed up butt naked. As long as I made it home alive. I'm okay," Goldie said as he opened the passenger's door on the red Corvette.

"You got so much heart, my nigga. I need somebody like you running shit with me. If that music shit doesn't work out, you definitely gotta spot with my squad," Head said as he leaned over to look up at Goldie.

"I'm definitely going to fuck with you, but remember the only color I bang is green," he said as he closed the car door.

"One hundred and I'm gonna get my people on that what we talked about A.S.A.P." Head pulled out of the circular driveway before Goldie even made it to the front door.

Goldie exhaled loudly and then started to bang on the door and ring the doorbell simultaneously. He was so nervous he didn't know what to do. He heard Jordyn ask who it was, but he didn't reply. She raised her voice and asked again; this time, she was closer to the door. He answered and said, "Me."

"Me who"? Jordyn replied from right behind the front door. She had her pistol at her side when she pulled open the door.

"Goldie, that's who," he said right before he saw her fall to the floor.

THE END...... TO BE CONTINUED!!!!

Also by Sevyn McCray

What Da Lick Read? The Triple Cross
The Real Blockwives of Atlanta: A Hustlers Dream
What Da Lick Read? 2 Beastmode
Love and Traphouses Atlanta
Love and Traphouses 2: Sleeping with the Enemy
L.A. to ATL: The Dollhouse
by Robin & Sevyn McCray

WWW.SEVYNMCCRAY.COM

www.ingramcontent.com/pod-product-compliance
Lightning Source LLC
Chambersburg PA
CBHW070704280626
47159CB00022B/2078